NO TRESPASSING

Longarm broke off in mid-sentence as a rifle cracked behind them and its slug raised a puff of dust between the hooves of Julia's horse.

They looked around. A half-dozen riders were coming toward them at a gallop. All of them carried rifles, and one of them shouldered his weapon while they watched.

"Hit it up!" Longarm called, digging his heels into his horse's flanks. "Zigzag along! It looks like old Don Esquival still ain't got over his mad!"

— TABOR EVANS —

LONGARM

AND THE
CROOKED MARSHAL

JOVE BOOKS, NEW YORK

LONGARM AND THE CROOKED MARSHAL

A Jove Book/published by arrangement with
the author

PRINTING HISTORY
Jove edition/June 1990

ISBN: 0-515-10334-9

PRINTED IN THE UNITED STATES OF AMERICA

10 9 8 7 6 5 4 3 2 1

Chapter 1

Longarm had not been able to get a close look at the man who'd let off the shot that whistled past his head, but at the moment that was not important. The simple fact that the man had chosen him as a target was all he needed to tell him that he'd struck pay dirt.

Only a few minutes had passed since he'd gotten off the train that had brought him from Denver to the little town of Sheridan, in Wyoming Territory, to start the case to which he'd been assigned by Billy Vail. He'd been given the job less than a half hour after the chief marshal had received a tip by telegraph that Stang and Clevar, two desperados high on the Justice Department's Wanted list, had been seen there.

Before reaching the protective wall of a building, where he now stood taking stock of the situation after the unexpected pistol shot had streaked past him, Longarm had gotten only a quick glimpse of the man who'd triggered off the slug. The one brief glance he'd had of his fast-moving attacker was enough to confirm the validity of the tip that had brought him to Sheridan.

He'd noticed no limp in the gait of the man who'd fired at him before disappearing around the corner of the building, which identified him as Stang. There was no sign of Clevar, Stang's outlaw partner, but Longarm accepted it as a foregone conclusion that the pair had not split up. He was sure that Clevar was somewhere close by.

Because the reputation of both outlaws dictated a good measure of caution, Longarm did not press his pursuit openly. He used a stratagem that had worked for him many times in the past. Instead of moving down the street in hot pursuit of Stang, Longarm sidled along the wall, heading for the street the building faced, the point where his quarry had disappeared.

Taking off his hat, he tilted the barrel of his Colt until its muzzle pointed to the sky. Then Longarm balanced the hat on the pistol's muzzle and slowly pushed his arm forward to carry the hat brim and his concealed revolver past the edge of the shielding wall.

A pistol barked somewhere along the street beyond the corner and the tobacco-brown Stetson sailed off the Colt's muzzle. Even before it hit the ground Longarm was dropping into a crouch. The veteran of many such encounters, he knew that the man he was after would be looking for him at eye level rather than at the height of a man's thighs.

He found his balance instantly and for a moment held himself motionless, poised on one knee. Then he pushed his gun hand in front of him, the corner of the building still shielding his head and body, and slowly tilted his head forward to look down the street.

Longarm got a momentary glimpse of the gun wielder before the man saw him. He did his duty by the rule book. Raising his voice he called, "I got you spotted, Stang! This is U.S. Deputy Marshal Custis Long! If you're smart, you'll give up! Now, throw down your gun and step into the middle of the street! It's your last chance to surrender peaceful!"

A shot cracked from a different direction before the man around the building's corner could move or reply. The bullet cut into the wall only an inch or two from Longarm's face. It sent a shower of splinters from the wood, but none of the slivers that spattered like tiny dry raindrops onto his tanned leathery cheek drove into his skin.

Longarm was not surprised by the shot. He'd known from the first that he'd be facing two gunmen, and now he'd heard from Clevar, the second of the pair. Judging from the sound of the shot, Longarm figured it had come from some point cater-cornered across the street inter-section. He swiveled in time to get a vague glimpse of a moving figure, but he'd moved too late to see the man clearly.

Longarm did not waste a shot on his invisible second antagonist, but returned his attention to Stang. Peering carefully down the street, he saw the outlaw on the street in front of him, twenty or thirty paces distant. Before Longarm could trigger off a shot, Stang dodged into a slit of space between two of the buildings that faced the wagon-wheel-rutted main street.

Twisting around and beginning to worm himself back-ward, Longarm edged quickly along the wall of the build-

3

ing. As he'd hoped but only half expected, an alley ran behind the buildings that faced the street, and he lowered himself again into a crouch as he approached it. A single quick glance told him that he was still sheltered from the sight of the fugitive.

Longarm quickly decided to gamble that the man's companion had found someplace to take cover after missing with his one-shot effort. Taking the few remaining steps needed to bring him to the alley, he ducked into the narrow slit. The alley did not run in the same fairly regular line made by the faces of the buildings along the street. None of the buildings' backs ended at the same point, so the alley was cut by a jagged mishmash of unevenly spaced walls.

Longarm's first glance along its length had told him that it offered a half dozen places where a fugitive could find shelter or concealment. The back ends of storage sheds and outhouses that formed the ragged line along the alley's length were ideal locations for a running man to hide.

Now Longarm's keen ears went to work. In the late afternoon stillness even a small noise could be heard for a good distance. The metallic clicking of a revolver being cocked somewhere just ahead sounded like a miniature crack of thunder. Though he could not locate the exact spot from which the noise had originated, just hearing the clicks was all that Longarm needed to bring him fully alert once more. He stopped moving, not wanting to warn Stang by giving away his presence with even the slightest noise.

Dropping to one knee, Longarm kept his eyes fixed on the narrow passage. He fumbled along the ground until his fingers encountered a sizable stone, which he picked up and lofted in a slingshot throw. The rock dropped with a loud thunk on the roof of one of the buildings beyond the point where Longarm suspected the fugitive gunman stood waiting.

Just as he'd anticipated, the sound of the stone falling drew the gunslinger's attention. Stang stepped into the alley as he turned to look for the source of the noise. While he was turning, Longarm followed him into the narrow, torturous passageway. He took two or three steps and stopped, his Colt leveled at the moving outlaw.

"Don't move, Stang!" Longarm cautioned. "Just pull up and stand still right where you are! You're covered, so don't try to turn around."

In spite of the warning, the gunman did not stop. He swiveled, walking backward now as he leveled his revolver while he was making his swift move.

Longarm triggered his Colt before Stang's turn was completed. The heavy slug from the Colt sent the outlaw staggering backward a half step. For a few seconds Stang held his precarious balance, then he began sagging and crumpled to the ground. The revolver in the desperado's hand dropped to earth even before his collapse was complete. He fell across the weapon and lay motionless.

Longarm had not forgotten the shot fired by Stang's companion, nor the direction from which it had come. Though he had gotten only a glimpse of the man who'd triggered it off, he was sure that the gunman had been Clevar.

Leaving Stang's crumpled body for later attention, Longarm retraced his steps toward the mouth of the alley. He stopped at its end and peered along the street in time to get a fleeting look at the shadowed figure of a running

5

man disappearing behind the corner of the building that stood at the alley's end.

Though he'd glimpsed little more than the man's churning legs, Longarm had noticed the slight limp that had marked his gait, the limp that had been one of Clevar's identification points mentioned in the records of the fugitives that Billy Vail had given him to study. Leaving the alley, Longarm ran along the building wall. He stopped when he'd reached its corner and peered around it long enough to make a quick survey of the cross street.

By this time Clevar had rounded the front of the corner building and was angling across the wide street. Glancing past the running outlaw, Longarm saw that the outlaw's objective was the hitch rail in front of a saloon on the street's opposite side, where three or four horses stood tethered. Only a half dozen buildings, most of them saloons and honky-tonks and gambling houses, faced the street between the saloon and open country.

Looking in the other direction, toward Sheridan's main business section, Longarm could see buggies and wagons on the street as well as a few pedestrians. Clevar had already reached the center of the wide thoroughfare. Now Longarm could see that he had a good chance to block the outlaw's escape. By changing his present course to a wider angle he'd be able to get beyond the saloon by the time Clevar reached the hitch rail.

Positive that Clevar would not risk turning and trying to ride to freedom through Sheridan's busy business district, but would head for the open country that began such a short distance away, Longarm changed the angle of his chase. He began running straight down the center of the wide street.

Clevar reached the horses and pushed between them to the hitch rail, where he started to untie the looped reins of the horse he'd chosen to steal. Longarm had no target now, for the escaping gunman crouched as he worked, using the horses' bodies as a shield.

Longarm kept running, staying in the middle of the street. He was almost directly across from the hitch rail when Clevar succeeded in freeing the reins of the horse he'd selected and began turning the animal's head away from the hitch rail. Longarm glanced ahead and saw that he'd almost reached a position where he could be sure of intercepting the escaping outlaw.

What he did not see was the domed surface of a small boulder that protruded above the street's graveled surface. His bootsole grated on the boulder and slipped. Off balance, Longarm tried to maintain his footing, but even his best effort was futile. He lurched forward and fell in an ungainly sprawl.

As he plummeted downward, Longarm twisted his torso and threw out his arms in an effort to keep his balance. He realized at once that any effort to stop his fall would be useless and brought his extended arms together in front of him to break the impact of landing.

As Longarm's hands hit the street's coarse, graveled surface his Colt was jarred from his grip. The weapon skidded along the road and came to a stop a foot or more beyond the reach of his outstretched hands. He did not try to get to his feet, but scrambled ahead on all fours as he tried to reach the revolver's butt quickly.

He was still inches from being able to grasp the weapon when hoofbeats thudded behind him, and at almost the same moment Clevar's pistol barked. The slug whistled past Longarm's ear and threw up a burst of sand and gravel that spattered stingingly into his face and peppered grains of sand into his eyes.

Blinded for all practical purposes, Longarm's fine-honed instincts ruled his moves. He dropped his head and let his body sag in an awkward and seemingly lifeless sprawl. The hoofbeats of Clevar's horse sounded as loud as thunder in Longarm's ears as the outlaw swept past him. The escaping killer did not fire again, but all that Longarm could do was to remain motionless while the hoofbeats passed and their thundering faded to a faint whisper in the distance.

Longarm lifted himself onto all fours, swaying gently as he blinked his burning eyes and shook his head, trying to regain his vision as the men from the saloon reached him. The crunching of their boot soles on the graveled street told him of their approach, but he paid little attention to the noise; he was still kneeling, blinking, trying to force his vision to return, when they reached his side.

"You all right, stranger?" one of them asked.

"Far as I can see, he ain't bleeding nowhere," another volunteered.

"Just shook up some, I guess," a third put in. "He taken right smart of a tumble."

"I'm all right," Longarm said. His voice was a bit grating, and he modified it at once before adding, "And I've got so much sand and grit in my eyes that I can't see."

"Well, don't try to rub it out," one of the men said, bending to grasp the hand that Longarm was raising to his eyes. "Cousin of mine done that one time and hurt his eyes so bad he was damn near blind all the rest of his life."

"I've got to get moving!" Longarm insisted. "The

fellow that just rode off is an escaped convict, and I'm a deputy U.S. marshal. My name's Long, and my job's to catch that fellow and bring him in. There were two of them. I had to shoot the other one. He's in the alley behind one of those buildings over there. You can get your constable or deputy or whoever you got here to take care of him later on.''

As he spoke, Longarm turned to indicate the place where he'd shot it out with Stang. Belatedly, he realized that he did not know which way to turn because the tears that still filled his eyes blurred his vision so badly. At the same moment he also became aware that the men around him were nothing more than blurred shapes, their features indiscernible even in the bright daylight.

''I guess you're right,'' he went on. ''I've got to have my eyes looked at by a doctor or somebody who knows how to clear 'em up before I can do much of anything.''

''Doc Soames's office ain't too far away,'' one of the men volunteered. ''If you'll hold on to my arm, I'll walk you over there and see if he can fix you up.''

''I'd be mighty obliged if you would,'' Longarm replied. ''And my Colt's laying around here somewhere close. I'd appreciate it if one of you'd pick it up and hand it to me.''

He'd barely finished speaking when he felt the butt of his revolver pressed into his hand by one of the blurry forms he could see only in silhouette. Nodding his appreciation in the general direction of the man who'd returned the weapon, Longarm holstered it.

''Whenever you're ready to go, I am, too,'' he went on. ''I don't want to let that outlaw get too much of a lead on me, because I got a pretty good idea where he might be heading.''

9

Longarm felt a hand close on his upper arm, and the man to whom the hand belonged said, "You come right on along with me, Marshal. Old Doc Soames takes care of my family's aches and pains pretty good, and I don't imagine he'll mind looking after you right away if I ask him to."

"You're either a lucky man or a very smart one, Marshal Long," Dr. Soames commented as he swabbed Longarm's wet cheeks with cotton to wipe off the drops of eyewash he'd used in flushing the grit from his eyes. "If you'd rubbed your eyes or tried to blink away the bits of rock that I got out with my feather tip, you might have blinded yourself."

"Well, you sure done a good job," Longarm replied, opening and closing his eyes experimentally, relieved that he could see clearly again. "Now if you'll tell me what I owe you, I'll pony up and be on my way."

"I don't charge men in public service, like yourself," the doctor replied. "I somehow feel I owe you gentlemen a debt of gratitude for the work you're doing to keep our country safe."

"Well, now," Longarm said, "I appreciate that, but whatever I pay out while I'm on a case goes on my expense vouchers. It don't come out of my pocket."

"If that's the case, then I'll just charge you my regular two dollars office-visit fee."

Digging into his breeches pocket, Longarm pulled out two cartwheels and passed them over to the doctor as he said, "One more thing, Doctor. I need to know where the livery stable's located."

"Turn right as you go out the door. It's just a few steps down the street. But I'm very curious, Marshal

Long. That outlaw you're after has had time to cover a lot of ground by now. How can you possibly expect to catch up with him in country as broken up and unsettled as this is?''

"Why, I don't figure it's going to be all that hard," Longarm replied. "If you've lived here very long, you're bound to've heard about the Hole in the Wall.''

"I've only been in practice here for a couple of years, but I've heard it mentioned as an outlaw's hideout. It just didn't occur to me that the man you're after would head for such a place. But isn't that a dangerous place for you to be going to?''

"Why, I didn't look to be going to no tea parties when I started out in this job of mine," Longarm answered as he headed for the door. "All I can do is try to run down that murdering scoundrel and do my best to bring him in. And no disrespect intended, Doctor, but I won't get no place just standing here palavering, so I'll say thanks again and bid you good-bye.''

After a chilly night spent curled up under the scant covering of a saddle blanket, and half a day's riding behind him, Longarm was both hungry and unhappy when he saw the blocky outlines of two or three buildings breaking the horizon ahead. He'd ridden out the last few tinges of daylight before stopping the evening before to make a dry camp beside the winding trace of a road that he'd followed south out of Sheridan.

He'd been reasonably sure that he'd find some sort of shakedown on the trace of a road that led south from Sheridan, but during the five or six years since he'd last passed through the broken rolling country it had obviously failed to draw any settlers who would provide

11

accommodations for travelers. Wherever Longarm looked, the land had been the same: jagged, distance-blued tops of mountains to the west, the gentler skyline of broad rolling prairie to the east.

Now, with the sun just past its zenith and beginning the descent that would eventually drop it below the ragged horizon, his stomach was complaining even more than it had before darkness had forced him to stop at the close of the previous day. He toed the livery horse to a faster gait and watched the buildings grow in size as he drew closer to them.

By their appearance, neither of the structures represented the defeated ambition of some cowhand who'd set out to become a rancher. Both were neatly painted, one white, the other a bright shade of pink, almost red. A space of twenty or thirty yards separated them. A dun horse moved lazily in the small pole corral that stood behind the white house, and a clothesline stretched from one of the corral's corner posts to the house that was close to it. A pair of Levi's denim jeans and a blue workshirt, both faded to the hue of a noonday sky, hung on the clothesline. Other than that, no sign of life showed in either of the houses.

Longarm reined off the road, pulled up his mount in front of the white house and swung out of the saddle. He stepped to the door of the house and knocked. For a moment or two he thought the house empty, then he heard stumbling footsteps approaching the door. It opened, framing a lanky man, thin to the point of ema-ciation. He was badly in need of a shave and smelled of whiskey.

"Howdy," the man said. He stood swaying slightly, blinking his eyes as he stared at Longarm, and when he spoke his voice was tinged with the fuzzy speech of too much drink. "You looking for somebody?"

"As it happens, I am," Longarm answered. "A man that calls himself Clevar. He'd've passed along here yesterday, the way I figure, heading south."

"Oh, him," the man replied. "Sure. He bought all the grub I could spare him, and when the son of a bitch left he took my little girl along with him. He didn't have much to say about himself, except that he was heading for the Hole."

Chapter 2

After his momentary surprise had passed, Longarm asked, "That's the Hole in the Wall you're talking about?"

"It's the only Hole I know about," the man said, frowning.

"That's as may be," Longarm replied. "But there's a place way over along the Snake River at the west edge of the Territory called Jackson Hole. And down in Arizona Territory they got a place folks call a hole in the wall, except it's only a big cave."

"Well, this one here's the real one," the man insisted.

"I ain't about to argue with you," Longarm said. "But maybe you better tell me more about this fellow that's up in the Hole in the Wall with your little girl. For openers, what'd he look like?"

"Mind if I ask what business it is of yours?"

"Official business," Longarm replied, taking out his

15

wallet and showing his badge. "Long's my name, Custis Long. Deputy U.S. marshal."

"Mine's Reardon. What kind of official business did you say brought you here, Marshal?"

"I'm after this man I asked you about. He's an escaped prisoner. I don't suppose he mentioned being from any-place special?"

"Well, now, come to think of it, he didn't," Reardon replied, frowning.

"Maybe you better tell me what he looks like."

"Just about anybody you'd run into anyplace around here. Kinda tall and lean and needed a shave pretty bad. Oh, yes. He had a sorta gimpy leg, stiff, if you get what I'm aiming at."

"That matches up all right with the fellow I'm looking for," Longarm said. "Did he give you a name to call him by?"

"Listen, Marshal, he didn't give me one damn thing except a half eagle to pay for what grub I could spare. That was most of a side of bacon and a few onions I had left from the last picking I done before I turned over my garden rows. Then I throwed in some dried-out spuds and two airtights of tomatoes and what was left of a sack of cornmeal that the weevils had already started working on."

"That sounds like a pretty good bill of groceries to me," Longarm commented. "But how'd your little girl get mixed up in the deal you struck?"

For a long moment Reardon did not answer. At last he said hesitantly, "Well, now, Nora ain't such a little girl no more. She's pushing twenty, and she's got a lot of the wrong kind of ideas, like having her own house. That's her's back yonder." He pointed to the small brightly painted dwelling. "I had to put it up for her because she couldn't get along with my new wife. You see, Nora's real ma died birthing her."

"That happens," Longarm said. "So she went off with this fellow you sold the grub to?"

"Didn't ask a by-your-leave or anything else. Just said he started asking her about how to get to the Hole in the Wall, and he couldn't seem to catch on to how to find it, so she was going to saddle up and go along to show him the trail."

"Going off with a man she'd never set eyes on before?" Longarm frowned.

"Well, that's just the way Nora is. Flighty, like her ma used to be. Anyhow, I built her that little house because she couldn't get along with her step-ma. Then damned if her step-ma didn't cut away and leave me. Nora never did move back, saying I'd likely marry again, and she liked the idea of staying put in her own house."

Longarm was silent for a moment, then he said, "From what you've told me, I better cut a shuck for the Hole in the Wall myself. What's the best way to get there?"

"You can go either one of two ways. There's a trail you could pick up about three miles down the road, but it ain't the easiest thing to find. Was I in your place, I'd keep right on this road till you hit a little wide spot called Kaycee."

"That's a town you're talking about, I guess?"

"Well, the folks that live there call it a town, but it's not much more than three or four houses and a saloon. The trail to the Hole cuts off to the west about a mile past it."

"It don't sound like that'd be real hard to do."

"Well, the Powder River cuts across the road just a

17

little ways beyond the trail to the Hole, so if your nag starts splashing you'll know you've missed it."

"If that happens, I'll just turn back and look till I find it," Longarm said.

"And you won't be the first man who's had to look twice to see the Powder River once," the man said. "But the road's good to where you leave it to get to the trail, and it's about the only trail leading off of the main road. You can't miss it, and it'll take you straight up to the gap you go through to get to the Hole."

"I'm obliged," Longarm said. He turned and started for his horse, then turned back and added, "I'm likely to run into your girl. Anything you want me to tell her?"

"Not that she'd listen to you any more than she would to me," Reardon snorted. "But maybe traipsing off with an outlaw on the run will learn her a lesson. You might tell her she's better off at home than anyplace else."

"I'll do that," Longarm replied. "And I thank you for the help you've been, answering all my questions. Now that I know a little bit more about the way the land lays, it just might turn out to be that you've saved me a lot of trouble."

Back in the saddle and riding steadily ahead, his horse rested after a brief stop, Longarm was suddenly aware of the urgent messages his stomach was sending him that it needed to be filled. He fumbled his packet of last-ditch rations out of his saddlebag and munched parched corn and jerky to satisfy his hunger, letting his mount set its own pace.

Longarm was still eating when he reached a drop-off he hadn't been expecting. Reining in, he studied the vast expanse of the huge saucerlike depression. It might have been the footprint left by some unbelievably large elephant, for it was almost circular in shape, and around most of its confining bluffs its walls rose with little slant.

Directly ahead of him the road began a zigzag course, angling sharply from side to side down the face of the gently curving wall. Here and there round-shouldered gaps of jagged crevasses yawned in its sides, marking the mouths of canyons that showed as slits breaking the undulating line of its wall.

In four or five places small shining streams trickled across the floor and joined in the distance to form a larger stream, though it was hardly big enough to be called a river. There were a few trees on the floor of the big canyon, only an occasional sparse stand of low-growing brushy firs and a few areas where stunted broadleaf trees rose above the high grasses.

Almost directly below him and a little way off the brownish-red surface of the road Longarm saw the tin-sheeted roofs of a few buildings spaced widely apart. There was no sign of life anywhere except around the buildings, where three or four horses and a couple of mules ambled in their idle grazing. He took the buildings to be those of Kaycee, the little settlement Reardon had mentioned.

By the time Longarm had completed his survey of the terrain below, he'd eaten enough to satisfy his hunger. Lighting one of his long thin cigars, he toed his horse ahead and started down the zigzags that the road described in its descent to the bottom of the big saucer. On the comparatively level floor, the walls of the big sink were even more impressive than they'd looked from the rim. The end of the zigzag road had brought him to within hailing distance of the buildings he'd seen from above.

19

"Hello, inside there!" Longarm called without dismounting.

A minute passed, and then another before the door of the nearest building opened and a man stepped out. He studied Longarm for a moment before he spoke, then asked, "You looking for somebody special, stranger?"

"I guess that'd be a fair way to put it," Longarm replied in a friendly tone. "Is this the place called Kaycee?"

"Folks call it that," the man admitted somewhat grudgingly.

"My name's Long, Custis Long. Deputy U.S. marshal out of the Denver office. I caught up with the man I'm looking for up in Sheridan, a prisoner that busted out of a federal prison back East, but he gave me the slip. I've tracked him here and I figure he's taken cover in a place called the Hole in the Wall."

"For all I know, he might be around here somewhere," the man replied. "But this place ain't like a hotel, where you got to write your name down in a book before you can get in."

"In other words, you ain't seen him," Longarm said.

"Not hair nor hide. But it ain't my business to know who's passed by here on the way to the Hole."

"Your not seeing him don't mean he's not around here," Longarm went on. "The reason I stopped was to ask the way to the Hole in the Wall place."

"Why, you won't have no trouble finding it. Just keep going on the road till you just about come to the river. Don't go across it, just swing off the road to the west. After you've been riding a little spell, start watching for two buttes that stand real close together. One's tall and has a flat top, the other one's lower and makes a hump.

20

Just ride right on between 'em. After you've wound around between the bottoms of them buttes for a little spell, you'll be in the Hole. You'll know it when you see it.''

"Thanks, friend," Longarm said with a nod when the man fell quiet. "Looks like you've told me just what I need to know, so I'll be on my way.''

Longarm had ridden for almost an hour before he saw the two humps he'd been looking for. Both buttes towered high above the general level of the rolling prairie he'd been traveling over, and at first glance he took them to be a single formation, though one end did extend higher than the other. They were the only high-rising features visible on the generally rolling landscape, so he reined toward them.

As he neared the point where the level prairie began a slow upslope toward the buttes, he became more and more certain that he'd reached his destination. However, it was not until he'd gotten almost within spitting distance of the towering formations that he saw the small gap that separated their bases. Then he could also see the faint vestige of the trail that ran between them.

Positive now that he'd found the right spot, Longarm reined his horse into the narrow passageway where the buttes began their abrupt rise. Between the high walls he was shaded by the bulk of the buttes from the late afternoon sun, and with its reddening glare no longer in his face he could see more clearly.

Reaching the base of the tall, flat-topped butte, Longarm twitched the reins of his horse to slow the animal to an even more deliberate pace as it stepped its way through the narrow gap, which was barely wide enough

21

to accommodate the animal. As he moved ahead he encountered a few spots in the winding passageway where on one side or the other his stirruped foot scraped against the high walls.

With a startlingly sudden abruptness the end of the torturous gap yawned widely and the vista of a high-grassed meadow met his eyes. Reining in, Longarm lighted a cigar while he relaxed in his saddle and studied the limited stretch of the meadowed area enclosed by the sheer and almost vertical walls that formed its boundaries.

A half-dozen huts were scattered across the floor of the oval-shaped enclosure. All of them were small, and only two had uniform walls of milled lumber. The rest had been jerry-built, made of whatever materials their builders had been able to bring into the Hole from outside, lengths of narrow slats off picket fences, squares and rectangles of tin that had originally been signs advertising chewing tobacco or patent medicines, weathered shingles, strips of canvas from tents or tarpaulins.

About half of the shanties had chimneys erected from stones held together with mud mortar or streambed clay. Stovepipes rose from the roofs or protruded from the walls of those which had no proper chimneys. Longarm's quick but thorough glances around the valley floor revealed that only one of the chimneys was discharging a thin trickle of smoke.

"Well, now, old son," he muttered into the thin still air, "it just might be you've struck it lucky. Looks like you and whoever's in that shanty where there's smoke coming out are the only ones around. And just sitting here staring ain't the way to find out."

Toeing his horse ahead, Longarm started toward the

22

cabin. He reined to a stop when he'd gotten within hailing distance. Certain of only one thing, that the little building seemed occupied, but not knowing who the occupant or occupants might be, he took the sensible precaution of pulling his rifle from its saddle scabbard and pumping a shell into the chamber before balancing the weapon across his legs.

"Hello, you in the cabin!" he called. "Open the door and come outside where I can get a look at you!"

After waiting for what seemed to be a long time with no answer to his call coming from the cabin, Longarm lifted the rifle and was starting to swing out of his saddle when the door opened wide and Clevar stepped out.

That the fugitive killer was moving sidewise, crab fashion, his right arm dangling behind him, was all the warning Longarm had or needed. When Clevar turned, bringing up the revolver in his hand, Longarm swung the rifle's muzzle around and triggered off a shot. The bullet sped true and struck the outlaw. Its impact slammed into Clevar's chest and threw him backward. In the outlaw's dying reflex his finger closed on the pistol's trigger and the gun barked, but its slug plowed harmlessly into the ground a yard or more in front of the forehooves of Longarm's horse.

As Clevar was twisted and knocked backward by the impact of the rifle bullet, he hit the cabin's door as he toppled and knocked it open. Framed in the doorway a young woman stood, her mouth wide open with the shock of her sudden exposure to violent death. She stared at Longarm, disbelief of what she'd just witnessed showing in the expression of shock on her face. She began to shake her head.

23

"Don't shoot me, too!" she pleaded. "I haven't done nothing wrong!"

"Why, you don't need to worry about me shooting anybody else," Longarm assured her. He was studying her while he spoke, knowing that she could only be Nora. "I was after that fellow laying there on the floor," he added.

"What did you have against him?" she demanded.

"It wasn't anything he did to me, even if he did try to shoot me when I first ran into him up in Sheridan yesterday. I was just doing my job."

"Your job is to kill people?"

"You took what I said the wrong way," Longarm replied. "I'm a deputy United States marshal, name's Custis Long. That fellow busted out of the federal pen, and I was sent to bring him back."

"I'm sure glad you caught up with him when you did, Marshal. I guess I played the fool, letting him talk me into running off with him before I knew anything about him. I didn't catch on at first to the kind of man he was, and when I did it was too late."

"He was a bad one, all right," Longarm agreed. "When I seen he wasn't about to come out peaceful and seen he was starting to throw down on me, there wasn't a thing I could do but shoot first."

Nodding thoughtfully, she asked, "But what about me?"

"You'd be Nora Reardon, I guess?" Longarm asked. When she nodded he went on, "It was your pa that put me on the trail of that outlaw you ran off with. I'd say the best thing you can do is go back home and settle down."

"But nothing ever happens at home!" she protested.

"After running off from your pa with that outlaw, you oughta be right thankful you got someplace to go back to," Longarm suggested.

For a moment Nora said nothing. At last she nodded. "I guess maybe you're right. But it's too late to start out today, it'll be dark in another hour or so."

"I was thinking that myself," Longarm agreed. "I'm hungry as a bear cub, and I still got to bury this outlaw. Suppose you stir us up a bite of supper while I'm doing that. Tomorrow, I'll ride with you back to the road and see you safe on your way home."

After the long, busy day he'd had Longarm was sleeping soundly in the shanty he'd chosen as his bunking-down place when the creaking of its door brought him instantly awake. He'd discovered earlier, when he first entered the cabin, that the door had no lock. His Colt in its holster was hanging on the head of the bedstead and he slid it free as he sat up on the lumpy straw-stuffed mattress.

"Nora?" he called.

"Of course. We're all alone in this place, aren't we?"

"We are unless some of the outlaws that use it for a hideout have shown up unexpected," Longarm replied. "Did you get roused up by a noise or something?"

"No. I just couldn't get to sleep."

Nora's voice was a bit louder as she replied, and when Longarm saw the slit of night sky outlining the door widen and vanish he knew that she'd slipped inside.

"And you figured I might like some company?" he asked as he replaced the Colt in its holster and watched her darkness-shrouded figure start for the bed.

"Well, wouldn't you?" she asked.

Nora had reached the bedside as she spoke and her

25

body was outlined against the darkness. Now Longarm saw that if she'd had on a nightgown or dress when she came in she'd discarded the garment while taking the few steps necessary to reach the bed. Although the dense gloom of the little cabin obscured her features he could see her dark eyes glistening, and against her ivory skin the rosettes of her full breasts and the triangle of her pubic curls stood out plainly.

A bit belatedly, Longarm replied, "Sure. Especially when the company's a pretty girl like you."

"Even if I came up here with an outlaw?"

"That's past and gone. Everybody makes a mistake now and again." As he spoke the bed creaked and Longarm felt the thin mattress sag a bit under Nora's weight as she settled down beside him. He shifted to make room for her.

"Don't pull away from me," she protested. "You know as well as I do why I'm here."

"You sure don't have to draw me no pictures," Longarm agreed.

His voice showed his distraction, for Nora's fingers had gone at once to his crotch and started a squeezing, stroking caress. Nora did not reply because now she'd risen to crouch above Longarm's crotch and was caressing him avidly, her lips and her warm sinuous tongue supplementing the soft stroking of her fingertips.

Longarm did not say anything more, but lay back and enjoyed Nora's attentions. She prolonged her oral caresses for several minutes, then suddenly shifted to straddle his hips. He felt her fingers moving to position him, then she sank down on his rigid swollen shaft. She loosed a small ecstatic cry as she impaled herself and squirmed for a moment, then began to rock back and forth, crooning a wordless and almost tuneless moaning refrain while she twisted her hips from side to side in a slow deliberate rhythm.

Longarm lay passive, enjoying Nora's motions, until he felt her body beginning to shudder. Then he locked his hands in her armpits and swiftly reversed their positions. Driving deeply with a sudden lunge he held himself tightly against Nora. He did not move until her sighs and quivering had subsided, then he began driving steadily.

Small ecstatic sounds began bubbling from her throat almost at once, and as Longarm continued his rhythmic penetrations her body started shaking in an uncontrollable frenzy. Longarm kept driving lustily while Nora peaked and shuddered through her climax and her body sagged beneath him. He slowed the tempo of his drives then, but did not stop until she had risen to a second frenzy, and this time he joined her.

Long minutes ticked away before Nora sighed and stirred. "I never ran into a man like you before," she whispered. "But can you do it again in a little while?"

"Sure," Longarm assured her. "And afterward we'll get some shut-eye till daybreak. Then I'll see you get started safe on your way home. I'll have to head back to Denver right away, because I've spent more time closing this case than I figured to. And if I know my chief, he'll have another case waiting for me the minute I poke my head inside his office door."

Chapter 3

Within minutes of arriving in Denver on his return, Long-arm's prediction was proved correct. When the train hissed and rasped to a stop in Denver's Union Station he dropped to the station platform and picked up his saddlebags and rifle, then headed for the Federal Building. The pink-cheeked young clerk who presided over the outer office was not at his desk, but the door to Billy Vail's private sanctum was ajar. Before Longarm had time to drop his gear, Vail looked up. When he saw who had entered he motioned for Longarm to join him.

"I suppose you left those prisoners you recaptured at the city jail," Vail said. "I'll wire the warden that he can send a jailer from the pen to pick them up when he gets around to it."

"There won't be no need for that, Billy," Longarm replied, settling into the red-leather upholstered chair he favored. "I had to shoot one of them when they spotted me right after I got off the train in Sheridan."

"What happened to the other one?"

"Oh, he gave me the slip and got all the way to the Hole in the Wall before I caught up with him. He came at me with his pistol ready and aiming, so I had to shoot him, too."

"Well, put it all in your report and I'll have Henry make a copy for the warden at the pen so he can close his file on the two dead men," Vail replied. As he spoke he was leaning forward to scrabble through one of the stacks of documents that almost overloaded his desk top. "And I hope you got a good rest on the train coming back, because there's a new case that I'm putting you on right away."

"Don't I even get a chance to send my laundry out and spend a night sleeping in my own bed, Billy? I pay good money to rent that room of mine, but for all the use of it I get, I might as well pitch me a tent out on Colfax Avenue."

Vail did not answer at once. He'd found the file that was the object of his search and was scanning its pages rapidly as he flipped through them. He reached the last page, pushed the folder across the desk to Longarm and leaned back in his chair.

"You won't have to travel very far this time," he said. "Just to Santa Fe and maybe to Taos, and whatever other little bit of ground in New Mexico Territory you might have to cover close by there."

"It ain't always how far away the case is, Billy," Longarm commented. "It's the running around a man's got to do while he's working it. How much time do I have before I have to start traveling again?"

"Well, this isn't exactly what you'd call any sort of

30

an emergency." Vail frowned judicially. "It's a matter that's really outside our jurisdiction."

"Why're we getting into it, then?"

"Because Clem Briggs is mixed up in it. I don't suppose you knew Clem very well, but he was a fine chief marshal before he retired from this job I've got now."

"What's happened to him that he can't handle for himself?"

"You know that when one of us takes off his badge for good he's just a plain everyday citizen," Vail answered. "And I don't know all the ins and outs of it myself. But what I gather is it seems like the territorial authorities in New Mexico are giving Clem a pretty bad time over some sort of land dispute he's gotten mixed up in. He wrote me and explained that he needs help and I'm seeing that he'll get it."

"I take it that means I'm the help?"

"You take it rightly," Vail replied. "But let's wait to talk about it until after you've gone through the case file and are ready to leave. And since it's not a criminal case, I don't suppose that starting a few days late would hurt anything."

"I guess it comes down to what you call a few days and what I need to do. How many days are you thinking about, Billy?"

"Would you settle for four?"

"It's going to take me that long to get my laundry done and have my guns looked over," Longarm replied. "And then just about the time I get comfortable sleeping in my own bed again, I'll have to get used to another mattress in some fleabag hotel in Taos or wherever else I'll be going."

"Make it a week, then," Vail allowed.

31

"That's a real fair deal, Billy," Longarm said as he stood up. "And if you don't object, I'll just leave this case file with you right now. If I wait till just before I start out it'll all be fresh in my mind when I get to wherever it takes me."

Longarm blinked twice in the subdued light of his room before looking at the window, where slivers of brightening daylight were shining through cracks and tattered spots in the window shade. On the bureau beside the window the threads of light sparkled off a bottle of Tom Moore Maryland rye whiskey, and he wondered for a moment why he'd forgotten at bedtime to put the bottle in its regular place on the chair beside his bed.

Kicking aside the blanket, he stood up and stepped to the bureau, yanked the cork from the bottle and downed a satisfying swallow of the pungent rye. A handful of his long thin cigars lay strewn on the bureau beside the bottle. Picking up one of the stogies and a match, Longarm flicked his thumbnail across its head and lighted the cheroot. Only then did he step to the window and peer outside through one of the wider cracks in the much-worn shade.

Pale sunrise light flooding the narrow strip of fading lawn between his rooming house and the adjacent dwelling lifted Longarm's spirits. Another swallow from the bottle of Tom Moore completed his morning routine. Shirt, breeches and boots went on in their accustomed order, and the pistol belt that had been hanging on the bedpost was strapped on and covered by the long brown coat that had been hanging on the back of the room's other chair.

32

Longarm had laid his cigar aside while dressing. Habit led him to pick it up, but he clamped it between his teeth without relighting it. Then, donning his wide-brimmed snuff-brown hat, he descended the narrow stairway, opened the door and stepped out into the cool briskness of the morning's mountain air.

As Longarm walked with long leisurely strides toward the Colfax Avenue bridge, he noted that not only the rooming house, but the entire section of the unfashionable side of Cherry Creek where it stood, seemed to be still asleep. He crossed the bridge and turned east on the avenue. Ahead, the golden dome of the Colorado capital building was picking up the first rays of the rising sun.

Longarm rubbed his chin even though he knew he needed a shave, but George Masters wouldn't get around to opening his barbershop for another half hour. His stomach had begun sending him signals, so he walked past the dark windows of the barbershop to a little hole-in-the-wall restaurant. Perched on a stool at the counter he downed a generous meal of hotcakes, ham, fried eggs and coffee.

Leaving the restaurant twenty-five cents poorer but with a feeling of satisfaction glowing in his stomach, Longarm went back to the barbershop to become its first customer of the day. A quarter of an hour later, smelling of bay rum and tobacco smoke from the lighted cigar now clamped between his teeth, he pushed through the doors of the Federal Building and climbed the stairs to the second floor.

When Longarm stepped through the door of the federal marshal's office and saw that Henry hadn't yet arrived, he felt a momentary suffusion of virtue. Then he noticed that the door to Billy Vail's office was ajar and that the chief marshal was already on the job, fighting the paperwork that came from Washington in a seemingly endless flood.

Vail looked up, saw Longarm, and waved for him to come in. As Longarm passed through the door, the chief marshal glanced pointedly at the clock on his office wall and grunted. "This'll be the day the world ends. What in hell happened to get you here so early today?"

"Well, the week you gave me's up and done with," Longarm replied as he settled into a chair. "And I know how much store you set in me getting started to clean up that case you said was waiting for me down in New Mexico Territory, so I just came on in soon as I finished breakfast."

"I see," Vail responded. He scrabbled through the stacks of paper that crowded his desktop and came up with the thin file folder that he'd consulted when he'd first mentioned the new case to Longarm. He went on, "I'm going to show you this, but the minute you finish reading it I'm going to tear it up. I want you to forget—officially, that is—that you ever saw it."

"That sounds pretty serious to me, Billy," Longarm commented. "Just what the hell kind of case is this you're sending me out on?"

"You'll understand better after you've read it," Vail told him. "And I think you'll also see why I'm asking you to do something I've never asked one of my deputies to do before, something I hope I'll never have to ask one to do again."

Longarm took the file folder from Vail and read the first of the two letters it contained. One was very brief:

34

Dear Billy,

I've run into something that startles me and also makes me very angry because it can do a great deal of harm to the U.S. marshals' force. Billy, I'm an old man who'll never wear a U.S. marshal's badge again, but I want to be proud until the end of my days of the force we both honor and serve. If something should happen to me, I want this matter to be known by somebody I'm sure I can trust. I'd like to pass it on to you, but before I do I want your promise that you'll never reveal it except to one of our own in the line of duty. Please answer me at once and give me that assurance, and you'll hear from me immediately.

Cordially, Clem

While Longarm was reading a frown had grown on his face. He glanced up at Vail, but his chief's expression told him nothing. He took out the second letter, which was in a fatter envelope and showed signs of much handling. The script was identical with that of the first letter.

Dear Billy,

Though I knew you'd reply to my letter, I hadn't expected to hear from you so soon. I know you'll honor my request for secrecy. You're the only man I can think of who's in a position to do what I'm no longer able to. Here's the full story.

Some little time ago the last of my uncles died and left me his entire estate. I was surprised at the large sum of money which came to me until I realized that it represented the lifetime accumulation of all four of my uncles, each of them having made their brothers their heirs. This is beside the point, and I mention it only so that you will understand how I suddenly found myself a fairly rich man after scraping through life on the small salaries the government pays its workers.

For the past two or three years my niece, Julia, has been living with me, since I now need help in coping with most of the small details of daily life. When I learned of my substantial inheritance, it occurred to me that both our lives could be made much easier by moving into larger and more convenient quarters than my pension had enabled me to afford, and I began looking for a suitable home.

Without boring you by recounting the details of my search for such a place, I found one in the mountains north of Taos, the area which the natives here call the Rio Arriba, the "Upper River." This property was developed almost two hundred years ago as a monastery and later became a convent school. Today it is claimed by the Hinojosa family and seems to be under the full control of the family's patriarch, Don Esquival Hinojosa.

I say "seems to be" because when I began trying to buy the property, I could find no deed in the Taos branch of the land office transferring it to them. Don Esquival Hinojosa refused to meet with me, and when I persisted in my efforts by going to the Santa Fe Land Office to trace the title of the property, Frank Maltby, the land office chief here, tried

36

to discourage me from persisting to buy the property.

When I insisted on pressing my efforts to find out how the Hinojosas could claim the property as being theirs, I ran into a stone wall of silence. Don Esquival continued to refuse to meet with me, and when I persisted in trying to talk with him, Jason Tobin visited me.

This was a great surprise, because Tobin has not been at all friendly. When I moved here from Denver, I called on him as a courtesy that a retired chief marshal owed to one who was still active. He was cold to my gesture then and has avoided me on the few visits I've made to the office since settling here.

Again to my surprise, Tobin seemed quite friendly. He asked how I was enjoying retirement and we talked for quite a while about old cases that we'd handled, then in an offhand manner Tobin brought up the subject of my efforts to buy the Rio Arriba property. I described it to him and sketched my plans for it very briefly. Without going into all the details, when I'd finished he shook his head and remarked that in his opinion it would be a great mistake for me to press Don Esquival to sell.

I was completely taken aback and pressed him for the reasons that had led to his advice. During his hemming and hawing that followed, I got an impression that Tobin was avoiding the true reason for giving it, that he was acting because of pressures too strong to resist. The Rio Arriba country is a notorious outlaw haven. I have a suspicious mind, I suppose, but I sensed that some force which Tobin *could not resist was behind his visit. I'm sure that he would not have called on me except for an influence powerful enough to compel him to do so.*

Billy, we've talked of the problems and temptations which men face in our line of work, the efforts made to bribe someone in the jobs we're both familiar with. We've also talked about the ability we develop to smell trouble and crooked efforts even when there's no real evidence to support our hunches.

I smell crookedness and trouble in the chief marshal's office here, and you're the only one I feel I can trust and turn to. I'm not suggesting you do anything or asking you for more than advice about what I might do to keep our force from getting the bad reputation that some branches of our government have gotten in recent years. Think about what I've written and then let me hear from you.

Yours, Clem

Longarm folded the letter and replaced it in its envelope before looking up at Billy Vail. His expression did not change as he gazed at Vail across the chief marshal's littered desk.

"Well?" Vail asked. "How did Clem's letter strike you?"

"It hit pretty hard, Billy," Longarm said soberly. "I'd say he's afraid our outfit might go the way the old Indian Bureau did a few years back, and you know how that wound up."

Vail nodded. "Of course. It was the end of the Indian Bureau, and a lot of people who weren't mixed up in any of the crookedness got bad names that they had to carry the rest of their lives, even if they didn't have any part in the crooked work.''

"You think something like that could happen in our bunch, Billy?''

"That's the first thing I thought about after I'd read what Clem had to say in his letter. And I thought about a lot of things he didn't say, too.''

"Such as what?''

"For one thing, Clem didn't come right out and name names. He didn't bad mouth anybody in particular. And for another thing, he didn't ask for any help except advice.'' Vail fell silent, but before Longarm could speak again the chief marshal added, "I got to know Clem real well when he was in charge here, before I got promoted. If he hadn't figured I might lend him a hand he never would've written me that letter in the first place.''

"I can see what you're getting at, Billy,'' Longarm said. "And sure as God made little green apples you've been holding on to that letter till I got back.''

"I won't deny that. Clem didn't give me much to go on in that letter. I had to do a lot of thinking about it.''

"Meaning you ain't sure there was anything you could do? Or me either, if push comes to shove.''

"Something like that,'' Vail agreed. "But he must know things that he didn't want to put down on paper.''

"And you're sending me to find out about 'em. Well, you're the boss, Billy.''

"Don't keep reminding me of it. But just remember, I've got bosses back in Washington. The rules say something like this is an internal matter that has to be referred to them.''

"Is that what you're going to do?'' Longarm frowned.

39

"Would I be passing all this on to you if I was figuring on running to the bosses back East and letting them know I didn't have enough sand in my craw to do what's got to be done?"

"I already figured that out, Billy. When do you want me to leave for Santa Fe?"

"There's a through train to Lamy leaving at four o'clock," Vail said. "It'll get you there late in the afternoon. And there's an old case we handled out of this office for the Santa Fe office. I've dug out the file, it's been hanging fire quite some time and you're assigned to close it. That's the official reason you're going there. Your travel orders and expense vouchers will be ready, so stop in and get them on the way to the depot."

"You mean I'll have the rest of the day to get ready?"

"It'll take you some time to get ready to travel. Now get out of here and don't show up again until you're ready to pick up your papers."

Longarm twitched the reins of the livery horse he'd hired at the livery stable in Lamy after getting off the train from Denver. Knowing he had no need to hurry, he'd been letting his mount pick its own leisurely way over the rutted mountain trail that wound up the long grade to Santa Fe.

New Mexico's territorial capital was not high on his list of favorite places. On each of the several visits he'd made while working on cases that had taken him there he'd sensed tensions below its outwardly placid surface of mutual tolerance. Each visit had revealed to him more and more clearly the lingering, silently hidden three-way tug-of-war that was still being waged between the Indians and the descendants of the Spanish grandees who'd taken the territory from them and the Anglos who'd taken it from the Spaniards.

Looking ahead along the trail, Longarm frowned as he glimpsed a shadowy movement. He knew that the motion might have been nothing more than the flickering of a bird's tail or the scampering of a small forest animal startled by the thudding of his horse's hooves. He knew also that the movement he'd seen could equally well have been made by one of the bandits who specialized in robbing lone travelers making their way to Santa Fe from the railroad depot at Lamy.

A small cluster of dead brush was the closest thing to cover that he could see as he looked for a place where he could find shelter along the wide path ahead. Making the best of the small choice offered, Longarm reined over to it and dismounted. Tethering the livery horse, he pulled his rifle from its saddle scabbard and began walking slowly toward the spot from which the noise had come.

He'd taken only a half dozen steps when the faint scraping of boot soles on the hard soil reached his ears. The sound was so faint that trying to locate the direction it came from was impossible. Longarm stopped in the scanty shelter of the nearest brush clump and stood motionless. He'd emerged unhurt from too many scrapes in the past to ignore the edge given him by playing the patient waiting game.

Several seemingly endless minutes ticked away before his precaution paid off. The reward for his silent vigil came when another rustling noise reached his ears from the undergrowth ahead. While he was still scanning the brush in front of him with quick eye flicks, he slowly swiveled his head and the sound was repeated. This time it continued long enough for him to determine where it had originated. Shifting his feet a careful inch or so at a time, Longarm swiveled until he was facing the direction from which the noise had come.

As he peered through the brush he saw the dark form of a man holding a rifle emerging from the shelter of one of the tall pine trees that dotted the undergrowth. The outlined shape of the man ahead was all that he could make out through the bushes that covered the ground more densely now that he'd gotten some distance from the road. Longarm raised the muzzle of his rifle, but did not shoulder the weapon.

"Drop your gun and get your hands over your head!" he called. "I got you covered! You ain't got a chance to get away, so cut your losses and give up peaceful!"

A shot barking from the half-visible figure ahead was the only reply his shout received. Longarm responded with a quick unaimed shot from the hip without raising his rifle, but by the time his finger closed on the trigger the man ahead had turned to run, dodging between the boles of the tall pines.

Longarm realized that he'd have only the smallest chance to get in a telling shot in the few seconds when the fleeing man ahead would be visible in his dodging run from one patch of cover to the next. Without hesitation, he started running in pursuit of the fleeing figure ahead of him.

Chapter 4

"Whoever that sniper is, he sure knows the lay of the land," Longarm muttered to himself as he came to a halt in front of the stand of closely spaced pine trees where his quarry had disappeared. "But him popping into this tangle here might not make much never mind unless he figures on just holing up."

While he was standing motionless, Longarm kept his eyes busy scanning the bushes, but his ears were more useful to him than his eyes. Although he saw the tips and upper branches of the underbrush swaying now and then, the crashing of the invisible sniper thrashing through the tangled maze gave him the best indication of the direction the moving man was taking. Though he was never successful in catching a glimpse of the sniper, Longarm was soon able to judge with fair accuracy the point where the man would emerge from the concealment of the trees.

43

He resumed his pursuit, stopping for a moment now and again to listen and to study the telltale quivers of the treetops, which together with the crackling of the undergrowth marked the movements of his unknown adversary. Several times Longarm swung in a wide arc in the direction of the sounds, looking for a spot where he could circle back toward the unknown sniper. For several minutes his search was unsuccessful. He kept moving slowly to disturb the dry bushes as little as possible and at last saw an expanse of clear ground ahead.

Now it was possible to move more freely. The snapping of small twigs and branches reached his ears with greater clarity, and Longarm took advantage of the brush-free strip to sprint across it. He moved at a wide angle toward the noises that were still his only guide. Running in a fairly straight line, he crossed the open glade at a wide tangent to the more direct course taken by his hidden attacker, and gained the shelter of the pine stand that rose on the opposite side of the clear expanse.

Here the brush was thinner, the trees spaced farther apart. Longarm flicked his eyes around, studying the changed terrain. Only one long look was needed, for just beyond the edge of the small clearing some long-ago storm had snapped the bole of a giant tree. The break had not been a clean one. The top of the long-dead tree had not broken free of the bottom portion. It slanted down from the break's stump, leaning away from the thick base section of the trunk that rose above the ground at a height of five or six feet.

Longarm took the few quick steps necessary to reach the head-high stump. When he stepped behind it he discovered that the point where the fallen tree's thick trunk had snapped and broken was a mass of long, jagged, widely spaced splinters. It was now possible for him to stand erect and still be fully sheltered while he watched the terrain ahead through the slits between the stump's splintered top. He stopped and stood quietly, listening to the occasional faint sounds that came from the stand of trees he'd just left.

His wait was not a long one. Only a few moments ticked away before Longarm could see movement in the pine stand he'd just left. At first he was unable to make out any details, as the only things visible were the occasional small movements and the vague outlined shape of the man who was after him.

It was immediately evident to Longarm that the man pursuing him was still trying to find his trail. In the few moments when the stealthy sniper became visible as he dodged from tree to tree, Longarm noted that the man kept his rifle leveled and ready while searching the terrain with quick darting glances.

Secure in his own cover, Longarm decided to use one of the tricks he'd learned to throw someone tracking him off balance. Without showing himself, he raised his voice and called, "You might as well lay your gun down and hoist your arms high as you can over your head! I got you square in my sights, and if you try anything smart I'll pull the trigger!"

On hearing Longarm's voice the man tracking him dropped his rifle to a hip-shot position and began swiveling from side to side, scanning the landscape in front of him. He held his position for only a moment or two. When he saw no sign of Longarm in any direction, he dropped flat and started crawfishing toward the trunk of a fallen tree a few yards distant.

Longarm was quick to take advantage of the opportunity his unknown adversary had offered. He sent a bullet plowing into the earth a few inches ahead of the man's face. Then, to emphasize the advantage he now held, he followed the first shot with a second bullet that kicked up a spurt of dirt behind the prone man's feet.

"If you got any sense at all, you'll give up!" Longarm called. "My name's Long. I'm a deputy United States marshal, and I'm putting you under arrest!"

"I don't give a damn who you are! There's no way I'll give in, to you or anybody else!"

"If you got enough brains to fill a thimble, you'll give up, because it don't matter to me whether I take you in alive or dead!" Longarm went on. "You've had your chance, but now I got you square in my sights. If you don't give up, you're dead meat the first time you make a move without me telling you to! Now, toss that rifle away! Throw your pistol with it, if you got one! Then stretch out your arms far as you can reach and lay still. Do it now, because I'm running outa patience!"

A prolonged silence followed the ultimatum. When no shot came from the outlaw, Longarm's experience in similar showdowns with the lawless told him that he'd won the fight with words instead of bullets. He waited patiently, letting the hopelessness of the situation sink in to his adversary's mind. He was not surprised when the other man replied.

"All right!" he called. "I'll give in for now. But we'll butt heads again someday, and next time it'll be me that comes out on top!"

Although every move he made displayed his reluctance, the man on the ground obeyed Longarm's commands. He pushed his rifle to one side, then slowly drew his revolver and dropped it to fall beside the rifle. After an even longer delay he obeyed the instruction to roll over and lie down with both his arms outstretched.

"That's more like it," Longarm told him. "Just don't make no fool moves like scrabbling around to pick up one of them guns and you'll stay alive."

Longarm broke his own cover now. He stepped from behind the tree trunk that he'd used as a shelter. Without holstering his Colt or removing his eyes from the out-stretched sniper he walked slowly toward him. While still a step or two away, he hunkered down and gazed with cold eyes at his unknown adversary. Taking his handcuffs from the capacious side pocket of his coat he pulled his prisoner's wrists together and snapped the shackles on them. The job took only a moment, then Longarm stepped back and stood looking down at his captive.

"All right," he said. "Roll over now and let me get a good look at you." Longarm's eyes opened a bit wider when he saw the youthful face of his prisoner, then he remembered how young Billy the Kid had been when he started his career of outlawing, and he shook his head. He went on, "It's time you did a little bit of explaining. For openers, tell me who you are and why you set out to bushwhack me."

"That's a damn fool question," the prone man blurted. "Folks that're traveling on trains always carry a pretty heavy wad of cash. Taking it away from them is a lot easier way to make a living than punching cattle is."

"Oh, I'll grant you that," Longarm admitted. "But robbing them folks you're talking about—or anybody else, if you come down to it—is against the law, and it's my job to see that the law's kept. Now, I asked you if you got a name. I don't give two hoots in hell who

47

you are, but I imagine I'll find out when we get to Santa Fe. The only reason I asked is because it's easier to call you by a name than just point a finger and say 'Hey, you.'"

His voice sullen, the youth replied, "It's Parson. Sid Parson."

"That's more like it," Longarm said. "I've already given you my name. Now, get up on your feet, and we'll start on to Santa Fe."

"Now, wait a minute! Can't we settle this just between ourselves?"

"If you're asking can you buy me off, the answer's no," Longarm answered. "I know there's a few crooked lawmen that sell their badge, but you've picked the wrong man this time. Now, I've heard all the jawing I'm going to listen to. Stand up and let's get started."

Moving as slowly as possible, the frustrated young holdup man struggled for a moment trying to stand up without the use of his arms and hands. Longarm made no move to help him. He'd discovered long ago that any effort a lawman made to assist a captured criminal would be taken as a sign of weakness and often encouraged even a handcuffed prisoner to try for a breakaway.

"We'll move now," he told the handcuffed outlaw when he finally stood erect. "I left my horse back by the road where you jumped me. I guess you've got one hidden away in the brush, so we'll get it and be on our way."

"If I've got a horse—and I ain't saying that I have or haven't—you'll have to find it without my help," the young outlaw snarled.

"Well, now," Longarm replied. His voice was casual and unworried. "You're dead set on giving me as bad a time as you can, ain't you?" When his prisoner did not reply, but continued staring defiantly straight ahead, he went on, "Let's see, I figure I'd come about three miles from the depot at Lamy when you jumped me. Now that means we got a little more'n twenty miles to travel. I sure hope you got on a comfortable pair of boots, because if you ain't got a horse, you're going to walk to Santa Fe handcuffed to my stirrup."

"You wouldn't do a man that way!"

"If he's one like you're turning out to be, I would. Just try me, if you're dead set on finding out."

For a moment the outlaw was silent. Then he nodded and said, "All right, you win this hand, too. I'll show you where my horse is tethered. But you better not forget me, Marshal. I'll be getting even with you later."

"Just about every little jackleg crook I haul off to jail tells me something like that," Longarm replied as they started moving. His voice was flat. "So save your breath till you've got something useful to say, like where your horse is hidden. It ain't getting no earlier, and we got a long ride ahead of us."

Longarm and his prisoner had been riding in silence for almost three hours through the black moonless night that followed a purple and crimson sunset. Now as they reached the crest of a long, torturous, and slow ride upslope, he saw a few pinpoints of light in the distance below and realized they'd reached the rim of the big circular valley in which Santa Fe nestled.

After Longarm and the thwarted bushwhacker had mounted and started for New Mexico's territorial capital, the young outlaw had apparently realized that nothing he said would be of any help to him. Until darkness settled down he'd remained silent, but after the blackness of the moonless night enveloped them he'd spoken a few times to warn Longarm of some hazardous spot they were approaching, a steep downslope ahead, a stretch of treacherous rocky terrain underfoot, or a place where the sinuous trail made a sudden sharp and unexpected turn.

Smothering in his throat the sigh of relief that he'd started to release, Longarm gazed at the scattered gleams that broke the blackness. He tried to recall the trail ahead, which he'd traveled several times before, but this time his usually retentive memory failed to respond. All that he could remember at the moment was that it was long and winding and could even be called treacherous in several places.

Turning to young Parson, who'd been silent during the last half hour of their slow uphill ride, he asked, "I guess you know where the Santa Fe jail's located? It's been a good while since I've had a case here, and I can't remember where it's at."

"I don't give a damn if you never find it," Parson snapped. "It's your job to take me there, so I'll leave you to do it by yourself."

"Well, now," Longarm said mildly. "There ain't that much left of the night, and I sure don't aim to waste any more time on you than I got to. I'll just take you along to the Federal Building with me. I'd imagine they've got a closet or someplace in there where you can sit handcuffed to a chair the rest of the night, if that's what you'd enjoy doing."

"You do what you want to," Parson replied. "In case you ain't noticed it, Marshal, I'm a big boy now. I can look out for myself."

"Oh, I've noticed you're what passes for a full-grown

50

man," Longarm told his prisoner. "But a pretty sorry one, if all you can find to do for a living is steal from somebody else."

"Why, you—" Parson blurted, then fell silent.

Longarm waited for him to continue, but as the minutes ticked off and Parson still said nothing, he realized that the young outlaw had thought better of the heated remark he'd been about to make. Turning his attention back to the job of keeping them on the trail in the darkness, Longarm fished one of his long thin cigars out of his vest pocket and lighted it. The red glow that brightened its tip each time he puffed lighted up his thoughtful craggy face as they rode on slowly down the zigzags in the steep slanting road toward the sleeping city below.

In the eastern sky a raggedly thin line of grey was bringing the promise of daylight before the hooves of the horses ridden by Longarm and his young prisoner thunked across the loose boards of the Santa Fe River bridge. The town itself was beginning to wake up, though the grey of dawn had not yet brightened the sky above it. Lights were glowing through the windows of the houses along San Francisco Street as Longarm reined into the alameda and started for the ramshackle Federal Building.

A few lights were already shining from its windows when Longarm reined in at the hitch rail and swung out of his saddle. He exhaled a small, almost inaudible breath of relief that the long ride through the darkness was finished at last.

"Like I told you a while back, I ain't going to mess with you any longer than it takes to be sure you're locked up safe and sound in jail," he told young Parson as he

51

loosened the saddle strings that he'd used to lash his prisoner's feet in the stirrups. "Even if it was me that arrested you, I don't aim to wait around here till you go on trial. Right now, I'm going to put you in the charge of the U.S. marshal's office and have them take care of the red tape that'll have to be unwound before you stand up in front of a judge."

Longarm had not expected his prisoner to reply, and was not surprised when the youthful outlaw merely grunted. Then Parson slid out of his saddle and began stamping his feet on the hard-packed earth in front of the hitch rail. He made no comment when Longarm led him into the building and up the stairs to the second floor. As Longarm had expected, lamplight gleamed through the frosted-glass pane of the door that bore the sign UNITED STATES MARSHAL—DISTRICT OF NEW MEXICO.

Tables took up most of the space in the long narrow room that they entered. At two of the tables men were busy adding sheafs of tape-bound papers to already bulging file folders.

They looked up when Longarm pushed his prisoner through the door and followed him inside. Longarm did not recognize either of the men who'd looked up from their work and were staring at him and his prisoner. He took out his wallet and flipped it open to show his badge.

"Name's Long," he announced. "Custis Long, out of the Denver office."

"Long," one of the men repeated thoughtfully. He and his companion were on their feet now, starting toward the door. "I know I've heard— Oh, sure! You're the one they call Longarm."

"I answer to it when somebody calls me that," Longarm answered. He extended his hand when the first of the two local deputies reached him.

"I've heard a little bit about you too," he said. "I'm Slim Brady."

"Frank Chalmers," the second announced. As he and Longarm shook hands he went on, a puzzled frown forming on his face, "You sure got here early. Or did you come in from Lamy last night after the town was all closed down?"

"This fellow here's the reason I came in so early," Longarm replied. "He tried to bushwack me a little ways outside of Lamy. I got there on yesterday's train and he jumped me a couple of miles down the trail after I'd started here."

"You wouldn't be the first one that's happened to," Chalmers said. "There's been a lot of that going on. It's not in our line, but we hear about it."

"Anyway, I managed to snag him into giving up," Longarm went on. "Says his name's Sid Parson. I'd imagine he could help stop them holdups, if he's of a mind to talk."

"That's the sheriff's jurisdiction, not ours," Chalmers pointed out.

"Sure," Longarm agreed. "But I've been up all night and don't aim to waste no time getting some shut-eye. I'd be obliged if one of you wouldn't mind handing this fellow over to the sheriff and telling him I'll stop in later on and do the paperwork that'll get him off my hands."

"That'll be easy enough," Brady said. "We've got a little holdover cell back of the courtroom. We'll just put him in it till one of us has time to deliver him to the courthouse."

"Fine." Longarm nodded. "Now I'm going to go find

53

me a room. I guess there's a restaurant around close by where I can get some breakfast before I turn in?''

"There's a little all-night hole in the wall at the corner of the plaza,'' Chalmers replied. "You won't have any trouble finding it. And I'll tell the chief you'll be dropping in later on, so you can be sure he'll be here."

"I'll likely show up about the time he gets back from his noon meal,'' Longarm said. "It wouldn't do much good for me to wait here for him, because right now I got a bad case of stupids and all I can put my mind to is getting some shut-eye.''

Noon had passed and the late afternoon was well on the way to becoming evening before Longarm returned to the Federal Building. Sleep and food had done their work, and his steps were brisk as he crossed the cramped lobby and mounted the stairs to the marshal's headquarters. The door to the chief marshal's office was closed and neither of the deputies who'd been on duty when he'd made his earlier visit was in the long narrow room. Its only occupant was a young Hispanic man who sat at one of the desks that had been unoccupied at the time of his earlier visit.

"You are looking for someone?'' the man asked when Longarm stopped just inside the door.

"Why, I sorta figured the same fellows I visited with this morning would be here,'' Longarm replied. "But my business is with Chief Marshal Tobin. Long's my name,'' he went on, taking out his wallet and displaying his badge. "Custis Long, deputy outa the Denver office.''

"Ah, of course!'' the young man replied, rising and extending his hand. "I was told to expect you. I am

Alberto Espinosa, Marshal Long, the office deputy.''

"Pleased to meet you," Longarm said as they shook hands. "I reckon they told you I'd be back?"

"Of course. But they did not mention the reason for your visit, though I believe one of them said you needed to discuss it with Chief Marshal Tobin."

"There's an old case both of our offices are mixed up in," Longarm said. "It never has been closed, and my chief figured the quickest way to wind it up was for me to come over here and talk to your chief."

"I see," Espinosa replied. "Then you should tap on Marshal Tobin's door. There is no one with him at the moment."

With a nod, Longarm walked the length of the room and rapped on the door. A gruff call, "Come in," sounded beyond the frosted-glass pane. Longarm opened the door and stepped into the chief marshal's office.

Even though he was seated behind his desk, Chief Marshal Jason Tobin could not be mistaken for anything but a bull of a man. His bulky body seemed too big for the chair he occupied, his head was the size of a small watermelon, his nose was like the crag of a fat oval boulder protruding from a mountainside, and his neck and shoulders as wide and thick as those of an overgrazed range steer's. His hands, spread out on the desktop, looked like the paws of a bear or a gorilla. The only features that did not match his size were his eyes, which were too small for his face and half hidden by puffy lids.

"You're Long, from Denver, I suppose," he said, an answer rather than a question. His voice was too sharp and thin to be coming from a man of his size. "I had a note from Billy Vail saying you'd be here. Didn't answer it because I figured that even if I wired him for you not to waste your time and mine by coming to Santa Fe, you'd already have left.''

Although he was surprised by Tobin's abruptness, Longarm did not let his face reveal his feelings. He replied in the deceptively mild tone that had served him so well on many occasions. "I guess I don't follow you, Chief Tobin," he said. "Billy Vail wouldn't've sent me here without having a pretty good reason to."

"From his letter, you came here to close a case that started out as a dispute over an old Spanish land grant," Tobin said. "There were a lot of cases like that, and they fell in our laps when the only United States law here was our outfit. But as soon as the federal land offices were organized they took jurisdiction. I dumped all our land rights cases on them."

"I guess Billy Vail didn't understand all about that," Longarm said. "You see, we don't get mixed up with cases like that in our office."

"Vail should've known what he was doing!" Tobin snapped. "If he'd been anywhere near half smart, he wouldn't've sent you here on a damned wild-goose chase. Now as far as I'm concerned, you can turn around and go right back to Denver. I don't want you mixed up in any kind of case inside of my jurisdiction!"

Chapter 5

For a moment Longarm stood silent, surprised at the intensity of Tobin's outburst. Choosing his words carefully and speaking very slowly, he said, "Well, now, Chief Tobin, there ain't no arguing about this being your jurisdiction."

"I'm glad to see that we agree on something," Tobin commented sarcastically.

"Trouble is," Longarm went on, "you ain't my chief. Billy Vail is, and he's the only man that can give me orders about how to do my job. When he sends me out on a case I can't walk away from it on nobody else's say-so. Not even yours. Not till my case is closed."

"Now you're being insubordinate!" Tobin snapped. "Refusing to obey the direct order of a superior!"

"Oh, I'll grant that you got rank and I don't," Longarm agreed. "If this was your case, I wouldn't be arguing. But what it comes down to is you and Billy are both chief marshals, and you can't order me not to do something he's sent me here to do. Now, if I were sitting behind your desk, I'd send Billy a wire and ask him to order me back to Denver, because that's what it'll take to get me to leave."

"Damn it, Long, I didn't ask you for advice!"

"Why, I wasn't giving you none," Longarm replied. "I was just saying what I'd do if I were in your shoes."

"Quit beating around the bush!" Tobin grated. He'd moderated his voice, though his face was still twisted with anger. "I've given you a direct order to get off this case and go back to your own office. And if you disobey that order, you'll find yourself in real trouble!"

"That's as may be, Chief Tobin," Longarm replied levelly. "Except you don't have the right to order me to do anything. Now, if you want me out of Santa Fe, you just show me an order from Chief Marshal Billy Vail calling me back to Denver. Because I came here on a case, and I don't aim to quit working it until I get an order from him to get off this case and come home."

"What the hell kind of answer is that for a deputy to give a chief marshal?" Tobin demanded. "It's insubordination! And deputy marshals can lose their jobs for it!"

Longarm held back the hot retort that first popped into his mind. He was silent for a moment, then he said, "It's too bad we don't see things the same way, Chief Marshal Tobin. Now, if you were my chief and gave me an order, and I told you I wouldn't do it, that'd be insubordination. This might be your jurisdiction, but the only orders I follow are the ones I get from my own chief."

"By God, Long, I'm warning you!" Tobin said, his

voice choked with rage. "If I give you an order and you don't obey it, there'll be hell to pay!"

"Any time you want to test me out, you're sure welcome to try," Longarm told the infuriated Tobin. "Now, I'm going to get outa your way and let you go about your business, just like I'm going about mine. I'll be looking in now and again in case there're any messages that come in over the government telegraph wire. If you feel like you got anything we need to talk about, I'm staying at the DeVargas Hotel. Otherwise, I aim to leave you and your men alone and I hope you'll do the same for me."

Before the red-faced Tobin could reply, Longarm turned and left the office. As he stepped into the outer office he saw at a glance that young Espinosa had heard at least part of the heated conversation he'd engaged in with Tobin. When he passed the young man's desk Longarm nodded and lifted his hand in a good-bye gesture, but before he could reach the door the young deputy called to him.

"Marshal Long! May I invite you to have a small *copita* with me this evening after I go off duty?"

"Why, sure. I like a drink myself before supper. I'm at the DeVargas Hotel, and they got a little saloon right off the lobby. How does six o'clock strike you?"

"That will be very good. I will be there."

Emerging to the street, Longarm stopped for a moment to light a cigar while he decided his next move, and even as he was puffing the stogie alight realized that he was overdue for a visit to Clem Briggs. He turned toward the plaza and circled it to the winding rutted path of Cerillos Road.

He set out with long strides along the narrow tho-

59

roughfare, glancing at the numbers of the few houses that bore them until he found the number Vail had given him. The house was a modest dwelling, built to the size and general pattern of most of those around it: brown adobe walls broken by wide windows below the protruding *vigas* that marked the roofline and formed the only accent of its face. Longarm rapped at the door and waited.

His wait was not a long one. A tall haggard-looking man with wispy white hair and a wrinkle-seamed face opened the door and asked, "What is it you want?"

"I guess I've found what I been looking for," Longarm said. "That is, if you're Clem Briggs."

"I am," the man said. Then the half frown that had puckered his brows cleared away and he went on, "Of course! You're Marshal Long, from Billy Vail's office in Denver! I've heard about you, of course, and wondering when you'd get here since I got Billy's letter saying he was sorry he couldn't make it himself, but was going to send one of his deputies to look into the situation I've been concerned about."

"That's right," Longarm replied. "And I'm the deputy he sent."

"Well, come in," Briggs invited, swinging the door wider and stepping aside. "I was beginning to think old Billy had forgotten me."

"Billy don't forget his promises," Longarm remarked as he entered and waited for Briggs to close the door.

"I'm sorry my niece isn't here to meet you," Briggs said as he turned back to Longarm. "But she had a visit to make."

"I'll likely get acquainted with her later," Longarm remarked as he followed the retired chief marshal into a small living room and settled into the armchair his host indicated.

"Of course," Briggs said nodding.

"I'd've gotten here earlier," Longarm went on, "but I was on a case up in Wyoming Territory when Billy got your letter—that'd be the second letter you sent him. And I walked into a little fracas at Lamy right after I started here from the train yesterday, or I'd've been knocking at your door last night."

"A fracas at Lamy?" Briggs frowned. "I thought the Santa Fe railroad bulls kept things quiet there. They always did when I was chief here."

"What I ought to've said was that it was on the road here from Lamy that I got jumped. That started a fracas, but it didn't amount to much. I gathered up a prisoner in it and delivered him to the fellows in the marshal's office here to hand over to whoever's got jurisdiction up at Lamy. The thing is, all that jumping around kept me from getting here until it was, well, too *early* to come calling on you," Longarm explained. "Then I wanted to get a look at Chief Marshal Tobin before I came out to talk to you, so that's why I'm so late."

"Well, I'm glad you got here, Marshal Long. But while we're on the subject, I'd be interested to know what you think about Tobin."

"That'd be quite some order," Longarm answered. "Me and him didn't exactly hit it off. When push comes to shove, I guess you'd say we had a little argument."

A smile had been forming on Briggs's face as Longarm talked. He said, "I hope you came out of it ahead of him."

"It wasn't really such a much," Longarm answered. "But he ain't the kind of man I'd like to be taking orders

61

from. Anyhow, that didn't have a thing to do with what I'm here for.''

"I owe Billy Vail for sending you," Briggs said. "There were things I wanted to include in my letter, but it didn't seem wise to put my suspicions in writing at this point."

"Well, in them letters you wrote Billy Vail, you hinted pretty strong that there might be some things wrong in the marshal's office here, or at least that's the way him and me both took what you said. That's what Billy sent me to find out about, so why don't you do the talking for a while, and I'll settle back to listen."

Briggs sat silently for several moments, frowning thoughtfully. At last he began, "It's a little bit hard to put my suspicions into words, Marshal Long—" He stopped short and said, "You know, ever since I began hearing about you, I've thought of you as Longarm. Do you mind if I—"

"Not a bit," Longarm broke in. "I answer to it quicker'n I do my right name."

Nodding, Briggs went on, "I don't have a shred of evidence to support the suspicions I have, and certainly nothing that could be brought up in court to prove what I believe is going on."

"Maybe you better start at the front and take me along one step at a time," Longarm suggested. "Because Billy Vail didn't have much to go on, and I know I sure don't."

"What I think is happening here in the territory is the biggest land steal this country's ever seen. If it's brought off, it'd beat buying Manhattan Island for a few silver shillings." When he saw the blank look that swept over Longarm's face, Briggs explained, "A long time ago, back on the Atlantic coast, a cagey old Dutchman paid the Indians about ten dollars for the island New York City's sitting on today.''

"I see," Longarm said. Then he went on, "A minute ago you was talking about stealing land. I take it there's some men here setting out to get a big chunk of government land without even paying ten dollars for it.''

"That's exactly what I'm getting at, Longarm," Briggs answered. "I don't have any way of proving my suspicions—not yet, anyhow—but all the signs are there.''

"But where does the marshal's force come into it?" Longarm frowned. "That's land office business.''

"Of course," Briggs agreed. "But if someone in our outfit—" He paused and smiled and shook his head, then went on, "It's hard for me to realize that I'm not still in harness.''

"I guess the feeling sorta grows on a man," Longarm said.

"It certainly does. Except that I'm not part of the outfit anymore," Briggs said ruefully. "Anyway, I've got a very strong hunch that Jason Tobin's one of the bunch that's in on the deal. So I did the best thing I could think of, passing the word to Billy Vail. And I'm sure that Frank Maltby, the land office chief, is as deep into it as Tobin is.''

"After being head of the marshal's office for such a long time, you sure oughta know what's going on. Question comes down now to how much of it you can prove.''

"What's been stopping me from pressing this thing is that I don't have a bit of proof that'd stand up in court. Just hunches, suspicions, guesses, whatever you feel like calling them.''

"Even hunches don't just pop into a man's mind without there being a good reason,'' Longarm put in. ''Least-ways, that's how it strikes me. Maybe you better tell me about 'em.''

Briggs was silent for a moment, then he said, ''Obviously Billy's told you about me writing him.''

''He done a little more'n that. He let me read the letters you sent him.''

''Yes, that'd be Billy's way. And I don't mind, since it was the quickest and easiest thing to do. Then you'll know that I've been looking for a bigger house than this one. And that I tried to buy a place up in the Rio Arriba?''

Longarm nodded. ''Someplace up above Taos, as I recall. And the old fellow that it belonged to wasn't about to turn loose of it.''

''Yes. That was some time ago. I've kept looking, because there are a lot of fine old places up in that part of New Mexico, built by rich families that resettled here from Spain or Mexico. Of course, it's the same in a lot of other places in the territory. The amount of land some of those first settlers got astounds me, hundreds of thousands of acres.''

''I don't reckon land was worth very much back then.''

''It wasn't, of course, but that's changing pretty fast.'' Briggs shook his head as he went on, ''I'm getting away from what I need to be telling you about.''

After a moment of thought, Briggs went on, ''Well, as I told you a minute ago, it started when I decided to find a place up in the Rio Arriba country that my niece and I could move to. And after looking around for quite some time I found just the kind of place I had in mind. It's an old estate that was settled by one of the first families to move here. There's a big adobe house on it, still in pretty good shape, and several of the rooms could be cleaned up for us to live in while I fixed up the rest of it.''

"So you set out to buy it?"

"First I had to find out who the legal owner was. I didn't want to go on wild-goose chases, so I started looking at the records in the land office there in Taos. I couldn't find any records of ownership there, but I was told the land was supposed to belong to a man named Don Esquival Hinojosa.''

"Supposed to? Are you saying it don't?"

"If it does, I couldn't find any records saying so. What's more, when I asked this Hinojosa about it, he refused to even meet with me.''

"So you began to get suspicious?"

"Wouldn't you have?" Without waiting for Longarm to reply, Briggs went on, "What I did was come back to Santa Fe to check the records of the main land office here. Well, not only did I not find any deeds or records showing Hinojosa as owner, but Frank Maltby pretty much told me to butt out and forget all about it.''

When Briggs paused, Longarm said thoughtfully, "It seems to me that somebody's out to pull the wool over somebody's eyes.''

"I thought so at the time, and I still think so," Briggs said. "Perhaps because after I made that search of the Santa Fe office, I had a visit from Jason Tobin. He said he'd just stopped by to see how I was getting along, but I've been retired for several years now, and he's never called on me before.''

"From what little I saw of him today, he ain't the kind to make a call on anybody that he didn't want something out of.''

"He's not. When he came to see me we hadn't been

65

talking five minutes before he started hinting that I shouldn't bother trying to buy the Hinojosa property. And I can tell you he got pretty nervous even mentioning it."

"So I take it that you never did get what you were after?"

Briggs shook his head. "I did and I didn't. After I'd stewed things over in my mind for a while, I went back to the land office and asked to look at their files, but they couldn't find out anything that would've helped me. It seems some of their files had been mislaid, and a lot of those files just happened to be the ones that had the information I wanted in them."

"So you ain't any further ahead than you were when you got the idea there was something crooked going on?"

"I wouldn't put it exactly that way," Briggs replied, speaking very slowly. "Even if I didn't find proof that what I thought was really the case, I did find enough clues to convince me that there's a group of people, some here in Santa Fe and some up in the Rio Arriba, who're setting out to steal as much of New Mexico Territory's government land as they can get their hands on."

"I don't guess there's any way you can prove Tobin is mixed up with that bunch you're talking about, is there?" Longarm asked.

"That's what I want to do, of course," Briggs said. "He's not alone in it, as I've told you. I'm sure that the land office chief, Frank Maltby, is as deep in it as Tobin."

"Stands to reason he'd have to be," Longarm agreed. "And likely some of the land office clerks'd have to be in on the deal. Even if they weren't, they'd likely know that some kind of crooked work was going on right under their noses."

"Well, Longarm, now that you know why I wrote those letters to Billy Vail, do you think we can stop the land steal?" Briggs asked. "I'll admit that it looks like a big job, but somebody's got to stop them."

"It's going to take some chewing at, that's sure as God made little green apples," Longarm said frowning. "And I need to do some thinking before we lift a finger. Now, I'm supposed to have a drink with one of Tobin's deputies in a little while. I don't know whether he's just being friendly, or whether he's got something on his mind that might tie in with what you've been telling me. There's an off chance it might, so what I better do is run along and meet him, and tomorrow you and me can sit down again. We'll need to do a lot of figuring, but between the two of us we oughta come up with something."

Back at the hotel, Longarm found Alberto Espinosa waiting for him in the lobby.

"Sorry I'm late," he told the young deputy marshal. "I was out talking to Clem Briggs and sorta let the time slip by."

"It is of no importance," Espinosa replied as the two men walked across the small cramped lobby to the barroom. "I have only been here for a moment myself. How is Clem getting along? I became a member of the force only a short while before he retired, but he seemed to be a very fine man."

"He's that, all right," Longarm agreed. "I don't know him all that well myself, but I'd be inclined to say the same thing you did about him."

They stopped at the bar for their drinks and Espinosa

gestured toward a small corner table as he picked up his change, saying, "We can talk there without anyone over-hearing us."

For a few moments after settling into their chairs the pair sipped their drinks in silence, then Espinosa said, "My chief seemed very displeased to see you come in today. I could hear nothing of what you were talking about, but I've learned that he speaks loudly when some-thing happens to upset him."

"Well, now," Longarm said, "he ain't the only man who does that. But I got to agree, he did get his dander up pretty good a time or two."

"Your business here is not my affair," Espinosa went on, "I am still the junior deputy in our office. But I have learned to enjoy the work, Marshal Long. I would like to continue to be a deputy marshal."

"There ain't any reason why you shouldn't be one till it's time for you to retire," Longarm replied. "Unless you make some kinda bonehead play that gets you into trouble with your chief, or you get mixed up in some kinda crookedness that'd get you fired off your job."

"So far I have kept from doing anything wrong," Espinosa said. "And I have a pride in my family name that will not let me do anything to violate the oath I have taken. But there is what you call crookedness in our office. And I am sure that Chief Marshal Tobin is the man responsible for it."

Chapter 6

For a moment Longarm could not believe he'd heard Espinosa correctly. Before the silence between him and his companion grew embarrassing, he said, "Wrong can mean a lot of things, depending on how a man looks at his job. Maybe you better tell me a little bit more about what you mean by crookedness."

The young deputy marshal remained silent, a worried frown crinkling his brow. At last he replied, "I believe it to be bribery, Marshal Long."

"Where'd you hear about it?" Longarm asked.

"I have heard nothing. This is a thing I have seen with my own eyes."

"You mean you actually saw Chief Marshal Tobin taking a bribe?"

"With my own eyes," Espinosa repeated. "I have seen him take money." Then he added quickly, "I cannot swear it was a bribe for something he was to do or perhaps

69

not do. Or he may have been collecting a debt owed him by the man who gave him the money. Such things as these, I could not know.''

"Since you saw the money change hands, you oughta know who he took it from.''

"I did not know the man he met,'' Espinosa said. "But the way it happened was so secretive that what I saw could have been nothing else but a case of bribery.''

"Where'd this happen?'' Longarm was frowning thoughtfully as he spoke. "And when?''

"It was in Pojoaque, less than a month ago,'' the young marshal replied. "Do you know where that small village is?''

"Sure I do. It's north of here, on the road to Taos. But how'd you happen to be there?''

"I had been serving warrants in Taos. It was late when I started back to Santa Fe, and I had not thought to eat supper before I left. Because I wanted food that I could eat in the saddle, I stopped at a *ventorillo*, a small tavern in Pojoaque where I knew I could buy burritos.''

"And that's where you ran into Tobin?''

"I did not run into him,'' Espinosa answered, shaking his head. "He was not there when I went in. There was a man I did not know sitting at one of the tables, he was a stranger to me. I know the tavern keeper well, so I went with him into the little kitchen to talk with him while he fixed my burritos. He was heating the tortillas and beans when we heard the door open and someone come in. My friend asked me to watch the stove and see that the food did not burn while he attended to his new customer.''

"That'd've been Tobin coming in?'' Longarm asked when Espinosa paused for breath.

70

"Yes, it was Chief Marshal Tobin," the young deputy replied. "He did not see me, and before I could step out and greet him he sat down with the stranger who had been there when I arrived. When I saw him do that, to interrupt him would not have been polite."

"I guess there were other places where Tobin could've sat if he'd a mind to?"

"*Seguro*, Marshal Long. The place is small, but it has four tables. He chose to sit with the man. I did not want to intrude on them, for the moment Marshal Tobin sat down they began talking."

"You being in the kitchen, I don't guess you could hear what they were saying."

"Unfortunately, no. They talked with their voices lowered and stopped only for a moment when my friend the tavern keeper poured drinks for them. As soon as he left the table they began to talk again."

"Still not loud enough for you to hear, I guess?"

"Never could I hear anything they said," Espinosa agreed. "But I was curious. I thought at first that the man might be an informant, but after he and the chief marshal had talked for only a short while the stranger took a small sack from beneath his coat and put it on the table in front of Marshal Tobin."

"Did Tobin open it and empty it out?"

"He opened it only to put one hand inside and take out some money. It was paper money, so I do not know what the amount was, since I could not see it well. Then Marshal Tobin finished his drink, put some coins on the table, and left."

"What about the other fellow, the one that'd passed the sack over to Tobin?" Longarm prompted.

"He waited for a moment, then he left, too."

"I guess you asked your saloon keeper friend about them?"

"Of course, in a very offhand way," Espinosa answered. "He told me that he did not know either Marshal Tobin or the other man. But he did say they had met there before."

"And from the way you've been talking, I'd bet you were smart enough not to tell him Tobin was your boss."

"I told him nothing. I have learned since joining our force that we often find ourselves in strange situations, Marshal Long."

"We do, for sure," Longarm agreed. "And there're times when you'll wanta kick your own butt for getting caught in 'em. I got a hunch there's been a time or two you've wished you hadn't seen your chief that time."

"Yes, I have had such a thought," Espinosa replied. "I somehow feel guilty myself because until now I have mentioned it to no one. Tell me, Marshal Long, what would you have done if you had been in my place?"

"There ain't no real answer to that, Alberto. And saying your name reminds me of something. I don't answer to 'Marshal Long' when I'm with friends. I got a sorta nickname—"

"Longarm," Espinosa broke in. "I have heard it many times. You do not mind if I call you by it?"

"Not a bit. Most of my friends do."

"I am glad you number me among them. And glad that I have told you what I saw, and you do not question my words. Perhaps you have had happen to you something of the same kind?"

"Oh, sure. There're plenty of crooks ready to pay us lawmen to look the other way while they do some sorta dirty work. Bribery's been around a long time, but it'll be a cold day in hell when I put money in front of my duty.''

"I have tried to decide what to do," Espinosa went on. "I thought of mentioning to Chief Tobin that I had seen him, but for all I know what I saw might have been a perfectly innocent transaction, a sale of property, or something of the kind."

Longarm shook his head decisively. "Not likely. If everything had been open and aboveboard, Tobin wouldn't've gone to the kind of place you're talking about to handle it. If the man that he got the money from was paying off some kinda debt, he'd've likely brought the money to the marshal's office. No, it was some sorta underhand deal, just like you figured."

"I am glad you agree, Longarm," the young deputy said with a sigh. "Knowing of it has been a heavy weight on my mind."

"Talking about a thing that's made you feel bad generally takes a lot of the weight away," Longarm went on. "Now, it just happens that one of the reasons I'm here is to see if there's more of the kind of deal you tumbled onto going on, and not just in the U.S. marshal's office."

"You are saying that Chief Marshal Tobin is under suspicion?"

"I ain't saying much of anything, yet," Longarm replied. "And I don't aim to say anything to anybody till I see how the land lays in two or three different directions. Now, you just keep clammed up about what you saw, and soon as I do a little more nosying around so my feet are planted solid, we'll have another talk."

• • •

Longarm waited until midmorning on the following day before returning to Clem Briggs's house. This time it was not Briggs who answered his knock, but a young woman. She could have been any age from the middle twenties to the early thirties. The gardening smock that she wore over her dress concealed her figure, but Longarm noticed that she moved easily and quickly as she stepped back while opening the door.

"You'd be Marshal Long, from Denver," she said before Longarm could introduce himself. "I'm Julia. You've likely heard my uncle mention me."

"Oh, sure. And I'm right pleased to meet you, Miss Julia," he said. "I guess Clem's around someplace?"

From the moment she'd opened the door, Longarm had been examining Julia with quick glances. She was a tall girl, with a bun of blond hair caught up in a ribbon at the back of her neck. Her features were pleasant but unremarkable: a thin nose slightly uptilted at the nostrils; high cheekbones and a firm chin; and light blue eyes under thin, almost invisible brows. Her smiling lips were full and glistening.

"Of course," she said. "He's out back tending our little kitchen garden. He told me you'd be here sometime this morning, but he wasn't sure just when. Come in, Marshal Long. I'll go call him while you're making yourself comfortable."

Longarm settled himself on the sofa and leaned back against its soft cushions. On his earlier visit he'd been too interested in talking with Clem Briggs to give a great deal of attention to his surroundings.

Though the room stretched across the entire front section of the house it was anything but spacious, and the heavy, old-fashioned furniture that had been crowded

74

into it made it appear smaller than it actually was. The divan on which Longarm sat had an unusually high back and dominated the low-ceilinged room. Two chairs that matched the divan stood flanking the small, domed adobe fireplace in the center of the side wall.

An oval dining table with ornately carved arched legs filled the chamber's opposite side, and a half dozen matching chairs lined the wall from the room's corner to the door that opened in its center. A red Turkey carpet with a design of white roses and green vines covered the floor. A smaller table stood below the high narrow window in the front wall, and in the corner beyond the table a stand with triangular shelves displayed an assortment of fancy china and glassware.

Longarm was still taking stock of the room when Clem Briggs came through the center door.

"Well, Longarm," he said, "I hope you're rested from your trip by now. I did some thinking last night after you left, and the longer I thought about what seems to be happening in the marshal's office here the more anxious I got to do something to stop Tobin before he gives our entire force a bad name."

"I lucked out and picked up a little bit of news," Longarm replied. "It wasn't anything that'd be grounds enough to bring Jason Tobin up in front of a hearing board or haul him into court, but enough so I'm going up to that Rio Arriba country we were talking about and do some poking around."

"You don't think you ought to start here?" Briggs asked.

Longarm shook his head. "It's too close to head-quarters here in Santa Fe. If I began asking questions and poking around it wouldn't be but a little while before word of what I was doing got back to Tobin. Then he'd shoot off a telegram to Washington, and they'd wire Billy Vail in Denver and ask what was going on, and Billy'd be in the soup for sending me into another chief marshal's territory.''

With a rueful smile forming on his face, Briggs nodded and said, "Yes, I know how that works, and I don't blame you. Well, when do we leave?''

"Now, I didn't say a word about 'we,'" Longarm replied hastily.

"You surely don't think I'm going to miss out on a case I started,'' Briggs shot back. "Maybe I'm retired, but I've put in a lot of years as a marshal and I don't plan to sit here and twiddle my thumbs while you're working on something like this!''

"Hold on a minute!'' Longarm protested. "Clem, you can't just up and go—''

"Like hell I can't!'' Briggs broke in. "I could give you twenty reasons why you ought to be glad I'm volunteering! Listen to me now, Longarm, and do some thinking. The big reason is that I know that Rio Arriba country and I know the language and a lot of the people up there as well.''

"I can't argue against that,'' Longarm admitted. "But—''

"No buts!'' Briggs exclaimed. "Just remember what I told you yesterday about the old hacienda that I tried to buy, and you'll realize what an open door it gives me.''

Longarm sat frowning thoughtfully for a moment before replying, then he said. "Maybe I got a case of the stupids today, but I don't see how it's got anything to do with you going.''

"Think about it a minute, Longarm! The people up in the Rio Arriba don't take kindly to strangers poking into their affairs. If you go up there alone, you'll find yourself wasting a lot of time knocking on doors and asking questions that those folks won't answer. When I was chief marshal here I sent men up there more than a few times, only to see their efforts wasted when they had to come back because nobody'd even tell 'em the time of day."

"I won't argue about that, Clem," Longarm admitted. "You and me both know that making a water haul now and then goes with the territory. Anyway, this wouldn't be the first time I've had to poke and pry."

"You still don't see what I'm getting at," Briggs said. "The people up there are used to seeing me around, first when I was the territory's chief marshal and just lately when I started looking for a place to buy. Because they know me, they'll tell me things you or any other stranger couldn't drag out of them with a double-yoked ox team."

Again Longarm was silently thoughtful for a moment or two before he said, "Well, I got to admit you put up a pretty good argument, Clem. If you feel like coming along, you're welcome to. I guess it's like the barrel said to the box, two heads're better than one."

Until now, Julia had listened to the exchange between Longarm and Briggs without comment. Both men swiveled to look at her with surprise when she said, "If you two think I'm going to stay here in Santa Fe by myself while you're chasing around in that beautiful Rio Arriba country, you're badly mistaken. I'm going along with you."

Longarm and Briggs both spoke at the same time and the result was a confused babble of words that were totally incomprehensible. Both stopped at the same time and sat looking at one another, then both started laughing. Julia looked from one to the other for a moment before joining their laughter. As it subsided she tried again.

"I didn't expect either one of you would agree, but I didn't think you'd find it funny because I want to go along."

"We ain't just going on a picnic, Julia," Longarm pointed out. "This is official business."

Julia nodded and said, "Let me give you something to think about, Longarm. Clem's right, if you go up there alone, you'll get nowhere. The people will be polite, but they won't answer the kind of questions you'll have to ask. They'll listen to your questions very soberly, but instead of answering them they'll just start talking about something else as though you never had asked them anything."

"Julia's making sense," Clem put in before Longarm could reply.

"But this case I'm working on—" Longarm began, and stopped short when Julia held up her hand.

"You have to let me go," she said, "if for no other reason than the fact that Clem and I have been looking for a place to buy up there. I promise not to interfere with your business, and if anything, I may be of some help."

Longarm was silent for a moment, then he nodded. "All right. Since Billy sent me here sorta private and unofficial, I don't guess I'm tied to the rule book. We'll all three go, and you can look for a house while I see if I can find out what Jason Tobin's up to."

Chapter 7

Ahead of the three riders the jagged line of mountain crests rose high and saw-toothed against the late morning sky. The peaks dominated the horizon from east to west, giving Longarm and his companions a hint of the rugged going that lay ahead. On both sides of the narrow winding uphill road—actually more trail than road—patchy strands of small, twisted-branch piñon trees dotted the otherwise barren brownish yellow earth.

"Maybe we'd better stop in Pojoaque and get a bite to eat," Clem Briggs suggested. "Because there won't be another place where we can buy a meal until we get to the fork of the road in Chimayo. It'll take us the rest of the day to get there, and we'll be doing the smart thing by saving our trail rations for later."

"I was aiming to stop in Pojoaque anyways," Longarm said. "That young Espinosa I talked to ain't been a deputy long enough to learn all his p's and q's. He left some holes that I got to fill up."

"It takes most of the new ones a while to start thinking like a lawman should," Briggs agreed. "What'd Espinosa do wrong?"

"It ain't that he's done something wrong, Clem," Longarm replied. "He just still ain't figured out that there's times when you got to ask fifteen questions if you want to come up with five straight answers. I ain't running him down or bad-mouthing the help he gave me, but I'd give a pretty to've been there myself when he saw Tobin talking to the fellow he was with in that saloon."

"You think it's a regular thing for Tobin and that man to meet there?" Briggs asked.

"Stands to reason," Longarm answered. "From what Espinosa told me, I got the idea Tobin didn't waste his time a bit. He acted like he was right at home. He went straight to the table where this fellow was and sat down and they talked a few minutes. Then soon as Tobin got whatever kind of package it was the other man handed him, he paid off the fellow and both of 'em hightailed it right away."

Julia had been silent, listening to the conversation between her uncle and Longarm. Now she said, "Maybe you can find out more when we stop in Pojoaque, Longarm. Unless we want to eat trail rations it's the only place where we can get a meal. All we'll be able to get at the trading post in Chimayo is jerky or bacon."

"Yes, I remember that Chimayo trading post," Briggs added, "and we certainly don't want to try it again. The jerky we got was hard as iron and the bacon was beginning to go sour."

80

"That's why my saddlebags are bulging the way they are," Julia went on. "I brought as much food as I could from home. Even the big trading post in Taos is only a little bit better than the one at Chimayo."

"Well, I got my regular trail grub in my saddlebags," Longarm put in. "I don't tote much, but there's enough to keep us from starving."

"Oh, we're not in any danger of going hungry," Briggs put in. "Up in this part of the territory there are plenty of deer and quite a few bears. If we find ourselves running short after we set up camp there we can always do a little hunting, or make a quick trip into Taos or buy grub from one of the little *ranchitos* that're strung out along the river."

"You know the country better'n I do," Longarm said. "It's been a while since I've had a case in these parts."

"I doubt that it's changed much for a hundred years," Julia told him. "I was raised here but moved away, and when I came back here to the territory to be with Uncle Clem, I couldn't see a great deal that was different from the way it had been when I left."

Before Longarm could say anything in reply to Julia's comment, Briggs broke in, "I'm sure that little cluster of houses up ahead is where the tavern you want to stop at is located, Longarm."

"That building that's just coming in sight around the road bend does fit the description young Espinosa gave me," Longarm agreed. "So we'll just go in and have a bite and see what else we can find out."

"I've got a different idea," Briggs went on. "Both of us have been on the force long enough to know that most of the time when you're trying to dig some information out of a witness or a suspect, you don't want or need anybody else around.''

"There ain't much question about that," Longarm agreed.

"Then suppose Julia and I just rein in here," Briggs suggested. "You ride on ahead of us. When you're through questioning the man who runs the place, step out and give us a wave and we'll join you."

"That's right thoughtful of you, Clem," Longarm said. "I guess if it's all right with you it'll be all right with Julia."

"I won't mind a bit," she assured him. "I'll be glad of a chance to get out of my saddle and stretch a bit before we eat."

Longarm took out one of his long slim cigars and lighted it as he toed his horse ahead. He reached the squat little adobe building that housed the cantina and stepped through its scarred and battered door. The description of the place that he'd gotten from Espinosa had prepared him not to expect anything fancy, but he hadn't thought it would be quite so small or so dingily furnished, or that the streaked whitewash on the interior walls would be patched in places with unpainted brown adobe.

His first quick sweeping glance of inspection revealed that the small structure was divided into two rooms. Mounted on the wall that divided them a thick, sturdy plank spanned half its length and one half of the end wall, and had obviously been provided for patrons who preferred to drink standing up. The section of the bar, if it could be called that, along the wall ended at a door that led to the rear of the building. Four tables, two provided with benches and two with chairs, had been squeezed into the small space that remained in the room.

Saucers to which candles had been fixed upright in melted wax blobs stood on all the tables.

An occasional rattle of cookware trickled through the door, and now and then a man's voice raised in song could also be heard. Though Longarm recognized the melody as being one he'd heard before south of the Mexican border, he could not put a name to it. Except for the singer, the place was deserted, as he'd hoped it would be. He crossed to the open door in the wall and looked into the kitchen.

A long shelf that spanned the narrow room's back wall was broken by a delapidated kitchen range. The tuneful cook who stood in front of the range was stirring some sort of spicy smelling mixture in a bubbling pot, and a second pot beside it was sending up a cloud of fragrant steam. He gave his stirring paddle a final twirl as he turned away from the range and saw Longarm's tall frame in the doorway.

"Excuse me, señor, but I did not see you come in," he said. "You stop for *la comida*, no?"

"I'll sure want some of it, if it tastes as good as it smells," Longarm replied. "But I'd like to have a little talk with you first."

"*¿Qué tal?*" the man asked. "A talk of what kind?"

"All I need to do is just get you to answer a question or two," Longarm replied. "It won't take long. Then you can dish up some food. I got two friends back up the road a ways, and it'll take 'em a few minutes to get here, so I ain't in no hurry."

"I still do not understand," the man said, shaking his head. "Who are you to ask me questions?"

"Why, I'm a law officer, but I ain't looking to arrest nobody right now," Longarm replied. He took the leather wallet containing his badge from his pocket and flipped it open to let the young cook get a glimpse of it as he went on, "You see my name on this badge here, it's Long, Custis Long."

"And I am Fernando Carvajal. I own this cantina."

"Right pleased to make your acquaintance, Mr. Carvajal," Longarm said. "Now, like I told you, I'm just here asking a few questions, friendly like, about some special business I came here to settle up."

"You are sure of this? I do not wish to harm anybody."

"Like I just told you, all I want is the answers to a question or two."

"Then ask them," Carvajal offered.

"An evening or so ago there were a couple of men in here," Longarm began. "I don't know who one of 'em was, but the other one was Jason Tobin, the chief U.S. marshal from Santa Fe. I imagine you'd remember seeing 'em."

For a moment Longarm thought that Carvajal was going to deny having witnessed the meeting between Tobin and the man whose identity he still did not know, then the proprietor nodded slowly.

"I know only one of the men you speak of," he replied. "Marshal Tobin I am to know all my life. He is the friend of my father's from the time when he was the sheriff in Santa Fe and my father serve as one of his deputies."

"And you're sure you've never seen the fellow he came here to meet?"

Shaking his head, Carvajal said firmly. "It is like I tell you, him I did not know. Marshal Tobin meets here

84

with other men, too. None of them I have seen in Pojoaque."

"These fellows he meets, are they always the same ones?"

"Some I see more than once, some do not come a second time. Why do you ask, señor?"

"All this has got something to do with a case I'm on, down in Santa Fe. It don't have a thing that'd concern your friends and neighbors here in Pojoaque."

"Ask more what you wish, then."

"How often does Marshal Tobin meet one of these friends of his?"

"One, maybe two times a month. But a month or more will sometimes go by when he will not come."

"And does he always get a package of some kind from 'em?"

For a moment the tavern keeper hesitated. Then he shrugged and said, "Many times. Maybe most. But maybe I do not see him sometimes, when I am so busy."

"Seeing as your family's old friends of his, don't he ever talk to you a while? Maybe tell you why he's come up here, or who he's come to meet?"

"He does not tell me of his business, señor. And I do not ask. But one time he has come here to drink a *copita* with the *mayordomo* from the ranch of Don Esquival Hinojosa."

"Meaning that he'd be working for Hinojosa?"

"Many men work for Don Esquival. He is the big rancher in the Rio Arriba. Even so far away as here from his ranch, we know this thing."

"These fellows that Marshal Tobin meets, do they ever come here to meet anybody else?" Longarm asked.

"Two times, maybe three."

"Would they be some of Marshal Tobin's friends?"

"This I do not know," Carvajal replied with another shrug. "They are men I have not seen before." He hesitated for a moment, then added, "One I do know. He is deputy that work for Marshal Tobin in Santa Fe."

"And how many times has he been here?"

Carvajal shrugged. "*Quien sabe?* I am too busy to count how many times, but he has been here enough for me to remember him."

"I don't reckon he told you why Marshal Tobin sent him? Or if Marshal Tobin sent him?"

Carvajal shook his head. "I do not talk to him. I know him only when I see him."

"But you're sure—"

Longarm's question was interrupted by the arrival of Julia and Clem Briggs. Carvajal looked at Longarm with a question in his eyes. Longarm had no trouble in understanding his wordless request.

"Sure," Longarm said. "You got to tend to your customers. But these folks ain't in no hurry any more'n I am, they're friends of mine. We're all traveling together, and I've been looking for 'em to get here. Besides, you've answered all the questions I could think of right now, so we'll just sit down together at one of these tables and you can dish us up some of that good-smelling grub you got cooking."

After Carvajal had vanished into the kitchen, Briggs looked questioningly at Longarm, who shook his head.

"I didn't get a whole lot out of him," Longarm said. "But I've found out his name's Carvajal, and he did come up with a thing or two that's right interesting."

"You don't waste any time when you really start digging in, do you, Longarm?" Briggs asked.

"I just try not to fritter away time when I'm out on a case," Longarm replied.

"Well, goodness!" Julia exclaimed. "Don't keep us waiting! What else did you learn?"

"Enough to be pretty sure that what your uncle guessed when we first got to talking about this case is about right. There ain't no way to prove it yet, but I got a hunch he gave us a pretty good lead without even knowing it."

"A lead to the Hinojosa family?" Briggs asked.

"About as good a lead as we're likely to get," Longarm answered.

"What's the connection, then?" Briggs asked.

"Real thin, right now. Sort of a fine thread."

"A thread's more than we've had before," the former chief marshal went on. "If we can pick up a few more threads to add to it, we just might wind up with a rope."

"Oh, we got more'n one thread already," Longarm said. "We know Tobin comes in here sorta regular to meet that fellow the young deputy told me about, and the fellow that runs this place said something I ain't told you yet. He remembered a time when another one of the deputies from the Santa Fe office showed up instead of Tobin to meet the man from up north."

As Longarm finished speaking young Carvajal returned with a laden tray. They fell silent while he was serving them, and then began eating. After the tavern owner returned to his kitchen, Briggs asked, "What about the man from up north?"

"Seems like he was some sorta muckety-muck from the Hinojosa spread up north," Longarm replied. "That's all I got outa him, but I figure it's enough to go on."

"He wouldn't even give you the man's name?" Briggs asked.

Longarm shook his head and went on, "That's all he'd tell me. I tried to get some names out of him, but he says he don't know anybody except the ones that come here from Santa Fe."

"Did you believe him?" Julia asked.

"I don't think he was lying," Longarm told her. "After you question as many suspects as your uncle and me have, you get to where you can smell a lie when you run into one."

"There's no use in trying to find out anything here, I guess," Briggs said.

"None that I can see," Longarm agreed. "We'll eat and push on to what you call the Rio Arriba. If we're going to find out anything, we got to be where the crooked work starts, and I figure that we've found out about all there is to dig up here."

Ahead of them the dark brown slope of the almost barren land still slanted upward when Clem Briggs reined in beside a small stand of piñon trees. Longarm waited for Julia to pull up her horse before bringing his own mount to a halt.

"We've got two choices here," Briggs said. "After we top this rise the trail forks. One branch will take us into Taos, the other one gets us to the river where Don Esquival's property starts."

"We won't be hurting for grub if we don't go into Taos to stock up, will we?" Longarm asked.

"We've got enough to carry us for a week," Julia told him. "If we stay longer than that, we'll need to go into Taos and get more."

88

"A week's a long time," Longarm commented. "I'd say our best bet's to push on, seeing as how we're this far. We better be finding out what sorta deal's going on between this Hinojosa outfit and Jason Tobin."

"I think you're right," Briggs agreed. "There's a lot of really rough country up here in these San Juan Mountains, and with our horses already tired we won't make very good time."

"Well, now, you and Julia already had a run-in with this Hinojosa outfit," Longarm said. "But him and me ain't locked horns yet. If we figure to stay a while, I'd say the best thing we can do is find a quiet spot to set up camp. Then I'll go on by myself to wherever the Hinojosa place is and see what I can find out."

"That makes good sense," Briggs put in. "But instead of making camp, Julia and I can stay in the building that used to be the Hinojosa's home place. It's not too far ahead of us."

"I'd like to look at it again," Julia said quickly. "I still haven't given up hope of persuading old Don Esquival to sell it to us."

Briggs shook his head. "I'm afraid that's a lost hope, Julia. But I don't see any reason why we shouldn't use it, or one of those smaller abandoned outbuildings around it."

"When you put it that way, I don't either," Julia agreed. "It's far enough away from the new Hinojosa place, we wouldn't be bothering any of old Don Esquival's people, and it's still in good enough shape."

"Let's head for it, then," Longarm suggested. "And soon as you get settled in, I'll go on by myself to have a little sit-down with this Don Esquival fellow."

"You don't really think you're going to get him to

admit that he's passing money to Jason Tobin, do you?" Briggs asked as they reined ahead.

"If it's honest money, he ought not mind telling me," Longarm replied. "And for all we know now, there ain't anything crooked going on between the two of 'em."

"But if it was honest money they wouldn't have any reason to be so secretive about it!" Briggs retorted.

"I said 'know,' Clem," Longarm reminded him. "You ain't been retired long enough to forget what kind of evidence we got to put up in front of a judge and jury to make a case that'll stand up in court."

"Oh, I haven't forgotten," Briggs said. "And the reason I wrote Billy Vail asking for help was that I couldn't swing the job of getting that kind of evidence without a badge to back me up. I could smell that something had gone wrong in the marshal's office, but I couldn't do anything about it."

"Now, you two've argued enough," Julia broke in. "And we're getting close to the old abandoned Hinojosa place. I want to enjoy looking at it without having to listen to a fuss."

They rode on in silence across the diminishing stretch of level land that lay between them and the mountains that rose in the distance. Here the terrain was relatively flat, expanses of grassland broken by a few small round-topped hillocks, and some areas where small stands of pine or piñon trees rose between the broad stretches of high, waving grasses.

"We'll be able to see the old Hinojosa house as soon as we get clear of the pine trees ahead," Julia said to Longarm after they'd ridden for a long spell in silence.

"That's all you're going to hear Julia talk about as long as we're around that old place," Briggs said to

Longarm, the chuckle that followed taking out any sting his remark might otherwise have had. "And I know she won't leave without making another try to buy it. Not that I object, but—"

Whatever he intended to say was forgotten as a rifle cracked from somewhere ahead of them and the slug sent up a small shower of earth in front of his horse's hooves.

Chapter 8

"Drop flat!" Longarm called to his companions as he whipped his rifle out of its scabbard and rolled from his saddle. He kept the reins in his hand and wrenched them with a twist to force his horse to drop to its side. Stretching out behind the shelter of the animal's body, he slid his rifle over the animal's belly, and waited.

A minute ticked away, then another, and Longarm peered cautiously over the side of his horse. From his new position he could not see Julia and Clem, but he heard them moving in the cover of a piñon clump a few yards away. He flicked his eyes over the stretches of open country ahead, searching for the sniper, but there was no second shot.

From somewhere close by, concealed in the waist-high grass, Clem Briggs raised his voice to say, "I don't figure we need to worry about whoever done that shooting. My guess is that he didn't intend to hit one of us.

93

We were clear targets, and anybody used to firing a rifle couldn't've missed unless they'd done it on purpose."

"That's right," Julia put in. "It was a warning that we're on Hinojosa land now, and uninvited guests aren't welcome. When we were here looking around for a house, the clerk at the land office in Taos told us to be careful not to get on the west side of the river, because that's where Hinojosa land begins."

"But we didn't cross any river on the way here!" Longarm objected.

"No, but we crossed two dry streambeds," Julia replied.

"So we did," Briggs agreed. "And it didn't occur to me before, but either of them might well have been one of the old Rio Grande riverbeds."

"Now, as far as I know there's only one Rio Grande," Longarm said.

"There's more than one, but only one's the big river we're talking about," Briggs replied. "That fool river's likely to change its course every time there's a big winter snow melt, or even a heavy rain."

"In my book a river ain't a river unless it's got water in it and stays where it belongs," Longarm snorted. "And I sure didn't see any water in them dry-bottomed gullies we rode across."

"New Mexico law's not like the law in other places, Longarm," Briggs replied. "There's not a lot of water—sometimes none at all—in some of these streams at this time of year in this altitude. And most of these old aristocratic families up here in the Rio Arriba still go by the old laws that they brought with them from Spain to Mexico."

Longarm snorted, then said, "Well, begging your

pardon in advance, Clem, it's one hell of a way to run a territory.''

"We'll find out real soon what the situation is," Julia said. "If I'm not mistaken, whoever let off those shots is coming up right now."

Even over their conversation the thunking of approaching hoofbeats could be heard now. A moment or two passed as the hoofbeats grew louder, then a man's voice called, *"¡Sostenese inmediatamente! ¡Quiero verles!"*

"You know more of the lingo here than I do, Clem," Longarm said. "But if I'm guessing right, that fellow's telling us to show ourselves."

"Oh, you're right," Briggs answered. Keeping his voice low, he added, "He's got to be one of old Don Esquival Hinojosa's hands. He wants us to come out where he can see us."

"This is your territory, Clem. Do we or don't we?"

"I guess we'd better. He's not likely to do anything except warn us we're trespassing."

"Well, we sure ain't got nothing to hide, and no place to hide in even if we wanted to," Longarm replied.

He was getting on his feet as he spoke. Briggs and Julia rose to stand beside him, facing the approaching rider. Though none of them mentioned it, they noted that the horseman carried his rifle resting across the rise of his saddlehorn where he could level it quickly. The man reined in when he was still a couple of yards distant and looked at them for a moment.

"¿Quién esta—" he began, then switched to a heavily accented English to repeat, "Who you are? And what you are do on Hinojosa land?"

Briggs looked at Longarm, a wordless question in his

95

knitted brows. Longarm nodded and Briggs turned back to face their questioner.

"Suppose you tell us who you are and why you feel like you've got a right to shoot at us and ask questions," Briggs said. "Then maybe we'll tell you, if you'll give us a good reason."

"I am Pablo Gomez," the man in the saddle replied. "I am *mayordomo* for Don Esquival Hinojosa. This is his ranch. You have no right to be here."

"How come we never saw you when my niece and me visited Don Esquival before?" Briggs asked.

"You are friends of *el patrón*?" Gomez asked.

"We know him," Briggs said. "And I don't imagine he'd take kindly to you shooting at us and holding us at gunpoint."

"How is it that I have not seen you before, if you and *el patrón* have the *amistad*?"

"Now, I didn't say that we was friends of your boss," Briggs answered quickly. "I said we know him."

"You do not say who you are," Gomez said. "And why you are look for Don Esquival."

Before Briggs could reply Longarm broke in, saying, "What my friend here didn't tell you is that I'm a United States marshal, and I'm here on official business. You'll be making a lot of trouble for your boss if you try to run us off or do anything else that'd keep us from talking to him."

"What official business?" Gomez asked suspiciously.

"Well, now," Longarm said, "that's private, between me and Don Esquival. If he wants you to know about it, he'll have to be the one to tell you. The only thing you need to know is that my business is with your boss

96

and I'm asking you to take us to his house or wherever he's at.''

"Don Esquival is tell you to come here?''

Longarm shook his head. "No. But I guarantee you that he's likely to be real upset if you don't take us to him.''

After a long moment of silent thought Gomez nodded. "I will do this thing, then. But you must ride in front of me when we go to the hacienda.''

"Don't worry, we ain't back-shooters,'' Longarm said as he and Briggs started toward their horses. "Just you tell us which way to go, and there won't be no trouble.''

Gomez nodded and reined his horse around. He waited for Longarm and Briggs to mount, then pointed toward a thicker than usual stand of piñon trees that stood at the end of the rolling meadow. "That way,'' he said. "Come, I show you.'' Reining his horse around, he started ahead of them.

Julia had been silent until the little procession started. Now she nudged her horse into the gap between Longarm and Briggs and said, "I tried to be just as inconspicuous as I could while you men were talking. Most Spanish men expect women to be seen and not heard.''

"I sorta figured that's why you didn't have anything to say,'' Longarm said. "It looks to me like Old Don Esquival keeps a pretty close watch over his ranch, the way this fellow up ahead popped up outa no place like he did.''

"This has been rough country since the Spanish first set out to open it up,'' Briggs said. "And that's been something more than three hundred years ago. It was pretty raw and ragged even before that, with the Indians fighting each other.''

"I'd still like to live up here, though," Julia said. "And I'm still unhappy because Don Esquival wouldn't sell us that big old house we tried to buy."

"Don't let it keep fretting you," Briggs said. "We'll find another one just as good, maybe better."

All three fell silent then as they followed Gomez through the stand of piñon trees. It was a larger and thicker clump than most, and the trail over which their guide led them was dim; it wove in and out in sharp and unpredictable zigzagged curves between the close-spaced trees. Gomez looked back at them often, as though to make sure they were still following him, and in a few places where the faint trail veered sharply he raised a hand to indicate the direction the dimly visible track would take next.

They'd just emerged from a stand of the thinning piñons when Julia exclaimed, "Oh, look! Over there!" She was pointing as she spoke. "That's the house I want so badly, Longarm! The one we've told you about!"

Turning to look in the direction in which Julia was pointing, Longarm saw the bulk of a massive adobe building that rose at the edge of a deep gully several hundred yards ahead. The big house stood beyond a broad stretch of beaten earth where the posts of abandoned corrals leaned in straggling lines, and the ruined crumbling remains of a number of small abandoned houses were visible.

It was obvious at a glance that the old main house would sooner or later join the small ones in crumbling to total ruin. Large gaps showed in its adobe-plastered walls where the protective layer of earthen plaster had cracked and crumbled and fallen away, to expose the tiers of adobe bricks that formed its walls.

Blue paint was peeling from the frames of the small windows that broke its facade, and in a few of the windows there were panes of glass cracked or broken. Wide deep splits had formed in the ends of several of the *vigas* that protruded beyond the line of the deep veranda of the entryway. In spite of the lack of care that showed in its appearance, the old structure remained impressive.

After he'd completed his quick inspection Longarm turned back to Julia and said, "Well, it's sure a right big old place, and I guess it was real nice in its day, but it'd take an awful lot of work to fix it up so's it'd be fit to live in."

"But that's one of the advantages of an adobe house!" she replied. "They're easy and inexpensive to repair."

"I'm afraid the house is something you're going to have to give up on, Julia," Clem said. "Don Esquival made it clear to us that he's not interested in selling it. And please don't start bothering him about it, because the case that Longarm and I are working on is a lot more important."

"Oh, I know that," she answered. "And I don't intend to waste any more time trying to make him change his mind."

During their conversation they'd slowed their pace a bit and dropped farther than usual behind Gomez. He turned in his saddle and saw the widened gap and called, "That is not the house to which we go! It is to the new one Don Esquival built only a few years ago. If I go too fast, tell me! I do not wish to be unfriendly, but you must ride closer to me!"

"We ain't trying to get away," Longarm called back. "Just keep on going and don't worry."

They rode steadily for another quarter of an hour before

99

getting the first glimpse of their destination. The new Hinojosa house was also built of adobe. It was even more imposing than the old one, and instead of rising many storys high it sprawled over an impressive expanse of ground. Its walls glistened with fresh whitewash and the blue paint on the window casements was glistening in the glow of the afternoon sun.

Corral fences and a large barn separated the main house from a straggling line of smaller houses. Children were playing around a few of the houses, and several women sat in chairs beside three or four of the small structures.

"That's quite some layout," Longarm commented. "It sure beats the old one by a country mile. Old Don Esquival must've struck it rich."

"Just as Jason Tobin did," Clem Briggs said slowly. "And even if we don't have any proof yet that there's a connection between them, I learned to be suspicious of sudden wealth and coincidences like that a long time ago."

They broke off their conversation, for Gomez was spurring ahead of them. He motioned for them to follow, pointing to the big main house. Falling in behind him, they reached the long hitch rail in front of the imposing structure and dismounted. Gomez led them toward the door, but before he reached it the door opened and a man dressed in a sober black livery stepped out.

"*¿Qué tal, Pablo?*" he asked.

"*Transgresadores,*" Gomez replied. "*Don Esquival encargome que llevar algunes de estos a la casa.*"

"*Sí,*" the liveried servant replied. "*Momento.*"

Dropping his voice as the liveried servant disappeared, Longarm said to Briggs, "I ain't too good at the lingo,

100

but I gather the boss man himself is going to give us the once-over.''

"It sure looks that way. But when he sees your badge, I've got an idea we'll be invited in.''

Before Longarm could reply, a tall man wearing the loose shirt and bell-bottomed trousers of a charro suit appeared in the doorway. His erect stature belied the age shown by his white hair and the lines and seams of his thin, jut-jawed face, which was drawn into a puckered scowl. The scowl became a look of surprise when he looked at Longarm and Briggs.

"Marshal Briggs!" he exclaimed. "Why did you not tell my vaquero that you were not a stranger to my home? He said you and your companions were trespassers!''

"Well, Don Esquival, we figured it'd be better just to go along with him,'' Briggs answered. "He was just doing his job, and we didn't want to make it rough for all of us. We knew you'd set things straight.''

"If you have come about the old house—''

"Not this time,'' Briggs broke in. "I just came with my friend here, to show him the way. He still wears his badge, but your range rider didn't seem to put much store in it. This is United States Marshal Long. He's from the Denver office.''

"Marshal Long,'' Hinojosa said, nodding at Longarm. "I must offer you my apologies, too. But Gomez is new on his job, and perhaps used bad judgment.''

"Oh, I saw right off that he was just doing what he was supposed to,'' Longarm said. "There wasn't no harm done.''

"I am glad you feel this way,'' Hinojosa replied. Turning back to Briggs he went on, "But you and your friends must come in.'' He paused for a moment before adding,

"The only thing I ask is that you do not again try to persuade me to sell you our old family home."

"No, Julia and me have given up on trying to get you to do that," Briggs replied. "Like I said, we just came along to show Marshal Long the way."

A frown forming on his face, Hinojosa turned to Longarm and said, "I cannot think why you have come here. I have broken no laws. But come in, we will go into my *sala* where we can have our conversation in private."

Standing aside, Hinojosa waved Briggs and Julia to enter. As they walked down the long cool corridor, he went on, "Since we are to have a business discussion, I will call Carmelita. She can keep company with you, Miss Julia, while we men attend to our own affairs."

"There's no need to disturb her," Julia protested. "I can walk around outside and look at the scenery while you're talking, or just sit in the *sala* while you men take care of your business."

"I insist," Hinojosa said firmly. He stopped at the open door they'd just reached and gestured for Longarm and Briggs to enter it. Then he went on as he turned back to Julia, "Come with me and I will take you to Carmelita's suite, it is just down the hall."

"I'd say old Don Hinojosa does pretty well by himself," Longarm commented as he and Briggs entered the room into which Don Esquival had shown them.

"From what I've heard, he's rich enough to afford to," Briggs replied. "He's one of the few ranchers here in the Rio Arriba who runs both sheep and cattle. They say in Santa Fe that he's got enough land to hold all the buildings and houses in Santa Fe and Albuquerque and still have room for a couple of good-sized Indian pueblos.''

Though the day was not especially cool, a small blaze danced in the domed adobe fireplace that occupied one corner. Armchairs stood in a rough arc in front of the hearth. A large mahogany desk with a matching swivel chair filled the space where the light from the room's three windows was best. The desktop was bare except for a penholder and ink bottle and a tray holding a decanter and glasses.

One wall of the room was taken up by small doors that could only belong to storage cabinets. A pair of well-used crossed long-swords and two shining new rifles hung on another. Three small watercolors decorated the third. The floor was covered from wall to wall with a red and white Navajo rug.

After glancing around the room for a moment, Longarm and Briggs stepped to the window. The view was the same familiar vista of rangeland extending to low craggy mountains that they had watched during most of the ride to the ranch. They gazed at the vista for a moment and were turning toward the chairs when Don Esquival came in.

''Please, sit down,'' he said. Indicating the tray on his desk, he went on, ''perhaps a small *copita* would refresh you after your long ride.''

''Well, now,'' Longarm said, ''there's only one time . when I say no to a drink, and that's when I'm on a case and a man that I might have to haul in to court offers me one. Meaning no offense, Don Esquival, but I got to beg off drinking your liquor till we see how the business that's brought me here winds up.''

For a moment the smile that had been on Don Esquival's face did not alter, then it twisted into an angry scowl. The old grandee said, "what do you mean by those words, Marshal Long? Do you accuse a man of my standing of committing some sort of crime?"

"Why, I ain't accusing you of a thing, Don Esquival," Longarm replied, his voice cool and level. "That's for the lawyers in the Justice Department to do, and they won't make a move till I've handed in my reports. All I came here for is to ask you a few questions."

"What kind of questions?"

"Before we get to that, the law says I got to warn you that I can stand up in court and swear that what you tell me now is what you really said, and I do that in front of a judge and jury."

"I am familiar with courtrooms," Don Esquival replied. His voice was strained and it was obvious that he was struggling to control his anger. "Ask your questions. I will reply or not, as I please."

"Well, to start with," Longarm said, "there's evidence that somebody's been passing bribe money to the territory's chief federal marshal in Santa Fe. I'll just ask you if you know anything about it."

"If someone has accused me of doing such a thing, it is a slander and a lie!" the old hidalgo snapped. "Let me face the man who told you this, and I will force him to tell you the truth!"

"Well, now, you might just get that chance," Longarm said, his voice still cool and level. "But I got another question or two that I'll need to ask you—"

Before Longarm could finish what he'd started to say, Don Esquival leaped to his feet. His face was contorted angrily and he shook his fist at Longarm. His voice was trembling with rage as he raised it to a shout and said, "No more questions! If you wish to arrest me, do so! But I warn you not to carry on this stupidity! If you do, I, Don Esquival Hinojosa, will see that you pay dearly!"

Chapter 9

Both Julia and Carmelita had been uncomfortable during the first few moments after Don Esquival introduced them. The old man had wasted no time on ceremony. He'd tapped at his granddaughter's door and opened it without waiting for her to answer his knocking.

Carmelita was still two or three steps away from the door when he opened it and Julia got the first glimpse of her impromptu hostess. She was a young woman almost as tall as Don Esquival, with a waterfall of glistening coal-black hair cascading down her back. Her thin, prominent, high-bridged nose was almost an exact duplicate of her grandfather's, as was her firm jawline and narrow face.

"Carmelita, my dear," Don Esquival said, "this lady is Miss Julia Meadows. She is related to one of the men in my office, with whom I'm discussing some business matters. You will please entertain her until my business with them is settled.''

Without giving Carmelita time to reply, the old hidalgo had turned and departed, leaving Julia and his grand-daughter staring wordlessly at one another.

Julia had been the first to break the awkward silence. ''I hope your grandfather didn't interrupt something that you were doing,'' she said. ''If he did, please don't let me keep you from going on with it.''

''Today is like most of my other days,'' Carmelita said. ''I have nothing to do that would be interrupted.''

''I'm afraid Don Esquival didn't give me much choice,'' Julia went on. ''He just announced that he was taking me to meet you and that you'd—well, he said 'entertain,' but I certainly don't expect you to—''

''Don't let my grandfather's ways embarrass you,'' Carmelita broke in. ''I'm used to them, and they don't bother me anymore. He's of the old school and thinks the only thing we women have to do is to obey men. Come in, Miss Meadows. I'm not doing anything that's at all important, and you're certainly welcome.''

Julia stepped through the door and glanced around. Though the sun's rays no longer came through the double window that was centered in the outer wall, the reflection of its brilliance through the bright thin outside air gave the room an impression of being sunlit. The room itself contributed to the illusion, for it was furnished with white-painted wickerware: two lounge chairs, a small divan in front of a domed corner fireplace, and a table along one wall. The light hue of the furniture and the white walls of the room itself seemed to bring brightness in from the clear outside air.

She sat down on the divan and Carmelita took one of

the chairs. For several moments neither of them spoke. Carmelita broke the silence by saying, "Please, don't feel that you're not welcome, Miss Meadows. Grandfather very often acts abruptly. He's used to giving orders to the servants. Except for the *capataz*—the foreman, you'd call him—and the *gerente* who attends to our office in Taos, none of them are educated. He sometimes speaks commandingly to me, but I'm used to it."

"I do feel a bit embarrassed," Julia admitted. "At home, my uncle treats me as an equal, and I must admit that your grandfather's commanding ways took me by surprise."

"But I'm used to them," Carmelita said again. "Now, let's sit down and get acquainted. Here on the ranch we're so far from everything that I don't often get a chance to visit with anyone except Grandfather and one or two of the younger women among the wives of the men who work on the estate."

"Yes, I can see why you'd feel a bit lonely, living so far from town, but I think I'd enjoy it, myself."

"Don't be too sure that you'd enjoy living this far from a town," Carmelita said.

"I'm sure that I'd enjoy it myself," Julia said. "Surely you have enough things to do to keep you busy."

"There aren't many things to do here," Carmelita admitted. "But I manage to find something to keep me occupied. Right now I'm trying to improve my painting."

Julia glanced at the white-painted furniture and tried to fill the conversation gap by saying, "You've certainly done nicely with your chairs and sofa."

"Oh, I didn't mean the kind of painting you're thinking about," Carmelita said. "I'm talking about artistic

109

painting, pictures. I started trying to draw likenesses of some of the children of our people who live on the ranch, but I'm not yet skilled enough for that. But I've done a few landscapes and outdoor scenes along our little river, and flowers and things of that sort.''

"I'm sorry I misunderstood," Julia apologized. "Painting pictures is something I don't know a great deal about. I'd like to see some of yours, if you don't mind showing them to me.''

Carmelita hesitated for a moment, then nodded. "Of course not. They're in a small room down the hall, where I paint when the weather is bad. If you'd really like to see some of them—''

"I would!" Julia broke in. With their original stiffness wearing off, she was beginning to feel more at ease.

"Then I will be pleased to show them to you." Carmelita was rising to her feet as she spoke. "Come, Miss Meadows.''

"Call me Julia, please," Julia said as she followed Carmelita into the corridor. "And if you don't mind, I'll call you Carmelita instead of Señorita Hinojosa.''

"If you wish, please do. I have very few first-name friends.''

As she spoke, Carmelita was opening one of the many doors that lined the wide hall. She motioned for Julia to enter first. The room into which she stepped was small and crowded. A wide table took up most of its floor space; both the tabletop and the floor were heaped with crumpled wads of heavy paper. Paintings, only two or three of them framed, hung crowded close together on both side walls. An easel with an unfinished painting on it took up a corner between the windows and the table.

"Oh!" Carmelita gasped. "I had forgotten how Luis

scattered his rough sketches and bad starts all over the place! You must excuse the room's appearance, Julia. Luis Velarte is the surveyor's draftsman. He has been working in here for the past several weeks, making new maps to replace the old ones that are now in the land office in Santa Fe. But I cannot be angry with him for leaving things in such a bad state, for he has taught me a great deal.''

''All the paintings on the wall are your work, then?'' Julia asked as she stepped farther into the room in response to Carmelita's gesture.

''Oh, of course,'' Carmelita replied, following Julia into the room. Kicking aside the wads of paper strewn thickly on the floor she stepped to the littered table and added, ''Except the maps and land charts. Luis did those. I have copied a few, because I need to practice drawing.''

While she talked, Carmelita reached over the table and began to smooth out some of the crumpled sheets. Julia stepped up to look at them. Both charts were colorful, displaying areas of hues shading from deep green to a lighter, more delicate hue of the same color, the other areas in which the color ranged from a light yellowish tan to a deep brown. Most of the colored areas were defined by blue borders that varied in width, others were outlined in black.

''You can see that these maps Luis drew are much better than mine,'' Carmelita went on, indicating the creased sheets of paper that she'd smoothed out on the tabletop.

Julia stepped up for a closer look. She had no trouble distinguishing the difference of craftsmanship in the drawings. In those made by the professional draftsman the hues of the colors merged in clean lines and the

111

shadings of green and brown were delicately colored within the wavering borders of black that separated them. Those which she took to be Carmelita's work were blotched and puddled, while the boundary lines had been drawn and erased and redrawn.

"I suppose that drawing and painting are hard to learn," Julia went on. "I've never tried it, myself." She picked up one of the crumpled sheets and looked at it a bit more closely. "And I'm sure that your friend is a painstaking workman. Except for those heavy pencil lines, this map is perfect."

"It appeared so to me," Carmelita agreed, "but Luis said that my grandfather objected to it because the lines were not true, they did not follow the ranch's real boundaries." She picked up one of the other crumpled maps and smoothed its creases before spreading it beside the first as she went on, "You can see, here and here and here, where he showed Luis how they must be corrected."

"Yes, the changes are quite clear," Julia commented. "They represent a great deal of land, too. I can understand why your grandfather wanted them changed."

"Luis complained a bit, not to my grandfather, but to me, in private, but he drew a new map, just as Grandfather had told him to. Because I was so eager to improve my own work. I watched him closely and made a copy of his while he was working. It's—" Carmelita broke off and began searching through the heaped and crumpled papers. She finally found the one she was seeking and laid it beside the map drawn by the draftsman. "You can see that I still lack the skill to do exacting work of this kind. But I learned a great deal, my next try will be better."

"It looks very good to me," Julia said, bending over the table to examine the drawing more closely.

Carmelita shook her head as she said, "Yes, but my colors aren't as true as his."

"Just the same, you've done a very fine piece of work," Julia insisted. "I think it's beautiful. It should be framed and put on your grandfather's wall."

"Since you admire it so greatly, the map is yours, Julia," Carmelita said with a smile. "Perhaps you will hang it on your own wall."

"But I can't accept—" Julia began.

"Of course you can!" Carmelita rummaged on the littered table until she found a hank of twine, broke off a length and was starting to roll the map into a cylinder when Julia spoke.

"I hope I can get it safely home without wrinkling it," she said. "I'll have to carry it in my saddlebag."

"That hadn't occurred to me," Carmelita said. Then her brow cleared and she added, "But it can be cured very easily."

She picked up one of the crumpled maps and smoothed out its wrinkles, then put the gift map on top of it and began rolling the two together.

"This old useless map will protect the good one and keep it from getting crushed," she said, reaching for the length of cord to tie the roll. "And the two of them together will be almost as sturdy as a stick of wood." Handing the cylinder to Julia she added, "Now it is yours to enjoy."

Julia did not protest further, she was familiar with the Spanish custom of making a gift of some object in their homes that a visitor admired. She tucked the rolled painting in the capacious pocket of her riding jacket as she replied, "Thank you, Carmelita. I really will have it framed and hang it on my wall."

"I'm happy that it pleases you," Carmelita replied. "Now let me show you—" She broke off as the sound of loud and angry voices burst through the opened door. Neither she nor Julia could make out the words, but there was no mistaking the tone of the voices. She whirled around, saying over her shoulder to Julia, "Grandfather and your friends are disagreeing! I must go and try to sooth him and get him to be calm before the argument grows!"

Carmelita ran from the room and down the hall, with Julia following closely behind her.

Neither Longarm nor Clem Briggs had been prepared for Don Esquival's sudden ill-tempered outbreak.

"Hold on, now!" Longarm said. He raised his own voice in order to get the attention of the old hidalgo. "Just because I got to ask you some questions ain't no reason for you to go off half-cocked!"

"Your questions are insulting!" Don Esquival snapped. "I do not wish to answer them! I will not reply to such a slander! You will leave my house at once, and you will not be welcome here again!"

"Don Esquival!" Clem said, raising his voice in order to get the old man's attention. "It's Marshal Long's duty to ask questions when he's investigating a case! He hasn't accused you of anything yet!"

"No, but it is quite plain that he intends to!" Don Esquival retorted. "I will answer nobody who comes into my house and then treats me as a criminal!"

"Now, let's all of us just take it easy for a minute while we cool down," Longarm suggested.

114

He was still facing Don Esquival, who had stopped at the end of his desk, but was still staring at him, his face twisted in an angry scowl.

"I will listen to no more of your slanderous words!" Don Esquival said hotly. "You are—" He broke off as Carmelita came into the room. His voice moderated as he gestured toward the door and went on, "Go back to your room, Carmelita! Alone! The woman will be going with these other two Anglos. They are not our friends, they have evil intentions toward us! I have told them to leave. I will not talk with them further!"

"Be calm, Grandfather!" Carmelita pleaded. "And tell me what they have said or done to make you so angry."

"They accuse me of bribery! They say—"

"Wait just a minute!" Longarm broke in before the old man could say anything more. "Like I told you a minute ago, nobody's accusing you of a thing right now, Don Esquival. You asked me why I came here and I told you I was looking into some things in Santa Fe that were against the law. Then the first question I asked, you busted loose, so I figure I was hitting pretty close to home."

"Even if you did not accuse me in so many words, what you did was equal to a threat that you would have me brought into court!" Don Esquival shot back.

"Now, that's as may be," Longarm countered. His voice was calm and level now. "But if you don't have anything to hide, it don't appear to me that you oughta get so upset."

Before Don Esquival could speak, Carmelita turned to him and said, "Marshal Long is right, Grandfather. I'm sure you have done nothing that should disturb you.

115

Please, be tranquil now and finish the business that brought him and his friends here."

Don Esquival started to say something, thought better of it, shook his head thoughtfully, and finally replied, "I have no further business matters to discuss with these Anglos, Carmelita, and I will have none in the future. If you will please escort them to the door, they can return to Santa Fe or wherever it was they came from. I will not speak with them again."

His jaw set and his obsidian eyes still glinting with anger, Don Esquival stalked to the door and vanished down the corridor.

Carmelita looked at Julia and shook her head sadly. She said apologetically, "Grandfather has a very short temper at times, and this is one of them. I'm sorry that things happened as they did, but you can see that I have no choice. I must do as he told me."

"I'm sure we understand that," Julia replied. She turned to Longarm and went on, "Don't you think the best thing we can do is leave? I know you and Uncle Clem didn't have time to finish talking to Don Esquival, but I'm sure he wouldn't sit down with you again."

"You're sure right about that," Longarm answered. "Looks like we might just as well pull up stakes and start traveling."

"Yes," Briggs agreed. "We won't be able to get to Taos before dark, but it's the closest place where we can get supper and a bed for the night."

"There's a shortcut you can take from here," Carmelita volunteered. "Our people use it all the time. It's an old trail, and steep in a few places, but it's still in good shape and easy to follow. I'm sure you passed the old family home on the way here—"

"Of course," Julia interrupted. "I fell in love with it, and Uncle Clem tried to buy it from Don Esquival, but he refused to listen to an offer—"

"It was you and your uncle who were asking to buy the old place?" Carmelita broke in. "Grandfather told me that Anglos from Santa Fe came to him with an offer, but I didn't realize it was you. All he told me was that he refused the offer."

"To our disappointment," Clem put in. "And I'm pretty sure I know the trail you're talking about. As I recall, it starts a little way behind the house."

"Yes," Carmelita agreed. "Since you already know how to find it, I won't waste time giving you directions. I'm afraid that Grandfather will be coming back soon. You've seen how short-tempered he is, and if he finds you're still here—"

"Sure," Longarm broke in. Turning to Clem, he went on, "Let's you and Julia and me mount up and ride. We'd best be cutting a shuck if we figure to get to Taos before midnight.

"That was one of the most astonishing visits I've ever made, I think," Julia remarked as they rode at an easy pace along the trail. "Carmelita and I were just getting well acquainted when old Don Esquival blew up."

"She's certainly a lot easier to get along with than her grandfather," Clem commented.

"I found her to be very nice," Julia went on. "She was showing me some of her paintings and sketches when his temper blew up. She insisted on giving me one of her pictures—well, not exactly a picture, but a plat map of the Hinojosa ranch."

"Now, why'd you want something like that?" Clem asked.

"You know how the Spanish are, Uncle Clem," Julia replied. "If you admire something of theirs, they almost always offer to give it to you. Just like they tell guests, '*mi casa es toyu*,' 'my house is yours.' "

"Sure," Clem said. "Custom of the country."

"Well, old Don Esquival don't seem to me like he'd give you much more than the time of day," Longarm commented. "And I ain't real sure he'd even go that far."

"Oh, he's an old devil, all right," Clem agreed. "And now that he's not likely to have much to do with us any longer, where do we look next for evidence that he's in cahoots with Jason Tobin in some sort of bribery scheme?"

"All I can see to do is keep digging," Longarm said thoughtfully. "We'll nosy around a little bit in Taos, see if we can find out anything from the bank there, like how much cash money that he takes out, and when. If we can get—" Longarm broke off as a rifle cracked behind them and its slug raised a puff of dust between the hooves of Julia's horse.

They looked around. A half dozen riders were coming toward them at a gallop. All of them carried rifles, and one of the men shouldered his weapon while they watched.

"Hit it up!" Longarm called, digging his heels into his horse's flanks. "Zigzag along! It looks like old Don Esquival still ain't got over his mad!"

Chapter 10

As Longarm shouted his warning he dug his boot heels into the flanks of his horse and the animal burst into a gallop. After taking a quick glance over his shoulder to make sure that Julia and Clem had responded to his call, he devoted all his attention to the landscape ahead.

They'd passed through the first strip of *chamisal* that stood between them and the road. Now they were crossing a broad stretch of high-grassed level mountain meadow that still lay between them and the low, ragged line of cliffs and small humped buttes that had to be traversed before they reached the road.

Longarm realized that their pursuers were mounted on fresh horses from the corrals at the new Hinojosa ranch-house and could probably overtake them long before they reached a stretch of terrain that might offer a chance for them to take cover in some sort of brush or trees. He thought back over their incoming ride, but could think of no place of concealment ahead for several miles except for the thin line of high growth that bordered the course of the dry riverbed.

A shot, then another, cracked from behind the trio, but by now both Julia and Clem had begun to follow Longarm's example. They were jerking their horses' reins from side to side, forcing the animals to veer wildly, offering targets that even the best marksmen among their pursuers found impossible to hit.

At the tiring gait they were being forced to maintain, the underworked and stable-softened livery horses soon began to breathe hard. Julia's mount stumbled once and broke its gait, but she managed to stay in the saddle and keep the horse moving. She could tell that it would not be able to maintain its headlong pace much longer. Glancing oover her shoulder, she saw that the range-toughened mounts ridden by Don Esquival's men were slowly closing the gap.

Longarm had already noticed the condition of Julia's mount. He twisted in his saddle and called to them, "Clem! Julia! How far are we now from that old Hinojosa house?"

Julia replied before Clem did. "It's not far, only about a half mile!"

"Then you and Clem take the lead!" Longarm went on. "Head for the old place! It's got good thick adobe walls, and hopefully we can hole up in it and stand off that bunch! You two just ride, I'll let off a shot at them fellows now and again, maybe slow 'em down a little bit!"

Both Clem and Julia responded at once to Longarm's direction. They urged the tiring horses to put on a fresh burst of speed, and the animals responded with enough of a spurt to force their pursuers to pay more attention to their own mounts. Julia and Clem were angling now toward the low ridges that marked the end of the flat stretch of prairie.

After the three had been on their new course for only a few minutes the vaqueros from Don Esquival's crew realized their intention. They changed their own direction, and began angling across the level expanse of open range on a course that promised to bring them quickly to the low, tree-capped ridges that marked the end of the wide swath of level, low-grass prairie.

Only a few minutes after Longarm and his companions had changed course, it was easy to see that the finish of the wild race was going to be a close one. Don Esquival's riders were as observant as Longarm and his companions. Looking back, Longarm saw their leader gesturing to his companions, pointing ahead and giving silent commands with waves and nods.

After he'd been watching for a moment, Longarm saw one of the riders sweep past the others and change course to an angle that would block the way to the abandoned hacienda. He watched the rider for only a moment before acting. Reining in, Longarm waited for a moment, until his tiring mount stood quietly. Then he slid his Winchester from its saddle scabbard and took quick aim before squeezing off a shot.

He saw the lone rider jerk in his saddle, then lurch forward and slide to the ground, where he lay still. Shouts rose from the fallen vaquero's companions. Two of them reined in and raised their rifles for aimed shots, but by the time they'd found him in their sights and triggered off their rifles, Longarm was on the move again, zigzagging across the short remaining stretch of level prairie.

He still had not caught up with Julia and Clem, but within minutes he'd reached a point where he could get an occasional glimpse of the old hacienda's brown adobe walls, spotting it through the high-growing strip of ungrazed range grass and the ragged line of piñon trees that stood in front of it. Longarm glanced back at the vaquero he'd brought down. The man still lay where he'd dropped from his saddle. His horse was now standing beside the fallen man, stretching its neck down now and then to nudge his prone master with its muzzle.

A shot cracked from the vaqueros, and dust spurted up only a few feet from Longarm's position. The first shot was followed by several more as Don Esquival's riders saw that Longarm was going to beat them to the thin line of stunted piñon trees that stood in front of the old dwelling.

Though a few of the slugs whistled by uncomfortably close to him and others raised dust puffs from the ground near the hooves of Longarm's tiring horse, none of them found a mark. He reached the line of vegetation and reined his horse through it.

Only a dozen yards ahead the age-blotched adobe walls of the old Hinojosa home rose abruptly beyond a strip of barren, well-beaten ground. Longarm had expected to see the horses ridden by Clem Briggs and Julia, but they were nowhere in sight. The front door of the big abandoned adobe house yawned open and Longarm headed for it.

"Get off and lead your horse inside," Clem Briggs called from somewhere within the house. "This room the front door leads to is big enough to hold a troop of cavalry.''

Though Longarm could not see Briggs, he dismounted and led his horse to the entry. The door had been removed from its frame, and although the livery horse he'd been riding stamped a bit nervously as Longarm led it through the wide opening, he had no real trouble getting the animal to follow him inside.

Clem was standing at the side of a wide glassless window that faced the area where the trail from the big meadow began. His horse and the one ridden by Julia were near the back of the cavernous chamber. Both were stamping nervously when Longarm led his horse back to join them, and when the three animals huddled together they grew calmer. Dropping the reins on the floor to ensure that the animal would stand, Longarm slid his Winchester from its saddle scabbard and stepped up beside Clem.

"Any of them fellows come in sight yet?" he asked.

Clem shook his head as he replied, "No. They weren't as anxious to catch up with us after you dropped that one who was riding in the lead."

Longarm glanced outside. The line of scraggly trees that he'd just passed through screened from their view the wide expanse of open range they'd just crossed.

"I don't imagine they've given up on catching us," he said. "They're bound to know the territory and they'd be smart enough to figure we've holed up in here."

"Yes, that makes sense," Clem agreed.

Longarm went on, "Old Don Esquival must've thought twice after we left."

"Meaning what?" Briggs asked.

"Why, I'd guess that after we rode off he figured that

123

if he let us get back to Santa Fe we'd start digging into whatever kind of crooked scheme he's into with Jason Tobin.''

"You're sure that's the reason?"

"Right now I ain't sure of anything except that there's got to be a reason for him sending them after us."

"That'd figure," Clem said. "But—" He broke off as Julia's voice sounded from the back of the huge room.

"I've looked around as much as I could in such a short time," she said as she came through the door. "I didn't see anything that's changed since you and I—" She saw Longarm and paused for a moment, then went on, "Longarm! You seem to've discouraged Don Esquival's men very effectively. If I—"

A rifle cracked outside the house. Its slug whistled through the glassless window between Longarm and Briggs and thunked into the adobe wall above the heads of the horses.

"Seems like they—" Longarm began, but broke off when another rifle shot sounded and the high-pitched whine of its bullet sang briefly in their ears before it thudded to a halt as it bored into the side wall beyond the door where Julia was still standing.

"Them fellows ain't giving up," Longarm went on.

He was pressing himself against the wall beside the edge of the window opening as he spoke. He dropped to his knees beside the bottom corner of the big rectangular gap in the wall. Taking off his hat he peered cautiously outside and ran his eyes along the screening trees as best he could without giving away his position to their attackers.

"Did you see any of them?" Briggs asked as Longarm

leaned back against the side wall of the room and levered himself to his feet.

"Not hair nor hide," Longarm answered. "But it stands to reason they've holed up someplace in that little strip of brush along the old riverbed. They'd know every inch of the ground here, seeing as how they got to be old Don Esquival's men."

"Oh, there's no doubt about that," Briggs agreed. "I'm sure there's not a single big rancher in the territory that doesn't keep a few expert gun hands around. That's a holdover habit from a couple of hundred years ago when the first Spanish settlers came to this part of the territory. They had to have some tough men because they were facing the Jicarilla Apaches to the east and the Utes to the north and the Navajos to the south."

"Sure, that figures," Longarm agreed. "So them fellows outside have got a sorta edge on us because they know the way the land lays better'n we do. But we got an edge on them, and we'd be plumb fools if we didn't use it."

"Maybe I see what you're getting at, but I might not be right just guessing," Clem said. "You mean going upstairs, I suppose?"

"I sure do," Longarm replied. "But not all three of us. Now, you and Julia have been in this big old house before, and I guess you've tromped over it pretty good."

"We certainly have," Julia agreed. "Every inch of it, not once, but twice."

"I sorta figured that'd be the way it was," Longarm said. "So, Clem, why don't you put a handful of shells in your pocket and find a window upstairs where you can get a good look at what all's going on behind them trees."

125

"That shouldn't be too hard to do, looking down on things," Briggs agreed. "And it sounds like a good idea to me. Even if I don't get a really good look at any of them, I can pretty well follow them by spotting places where the brush shivers or where the tree limbs are moving."

"Julia and me will be keeping tabs on them fellows from down here," Longarm went on. "There's a pretty good stretch of clear ground between the house and that line of brush. They'll have to cross that strip of open land to get at us."

"And as thick as the walls of this house are, they're going to have to come inside if they're really out to get us," Julia put in.

"There ain't no doubt about what they got in mind. And there's enough of 'em to rush us, all right," Longarm said. "Besides, whoever's bossing them fellows out there might get the idea to send a couple of men off a ways to circle around and come at us from behind."

"I hadn't given that any thought until now," Briggs said. A thoughtful frown grew on his face as he spoke, then he added, "Maybe I can find a way to get up on the roof. When Julia and I were looking at this place with the idea of buying it, the roof is about the only part of it that we didn't look at."

"Don't let's start jumping off of bridges before we try to cross 'em," Longarm suggested. "We're holed up here in about the best cover we'd find anyplace, and there's not too many men out there for us to handle. Clem, suppose you just head on upstairs. You'll be able to see any of them fellows moving before we do, so don't hold your fire."

"Sure," Clem agreed. He started to move off, then

126

turned and said with a small and somewhat sheepish grin, "You know something, Longarm? I haven't been in a fix like this since I had to retire from my old job. And I won't try to give you the idea that I'm not enjoying every minute of it."

"I won't go so far as to say I'm enjoying it," Longarm said with a grin, "but I ain't had a long spell of just sitting on my tailbone doing nothing, like you have. Now let's stop palavering and get ready to give them fellows out there what for."

Briggs nodded and disappeared through the doorway into the hall. Before the thudding of his boot heels on the bare wooden floor had died away, Longarm was striding back to the big window opening where Julia stood watching.

There was not enough room in the space she occupied for Longarm to stand beside her in the corner where the window joined the wall. He circled around the inner walls of the long narrow room and took up his old position in the corner opposite hers.

"I haven't seen a sign of movement," Julia volunteered as Longarm looked across the gap at her, his eyebrows raised in a silent question. "But I'm sure they've found cover in that strip of brush along the old river."

"There ain't much question about it," Longarm agreed. "But that don't mean they ain't worming their way toward us. That's what I'd be doing, if I was after somebody in a place like we are."

"I'm sure you've been in situations like this before, just like Clem has," Julia went on. "So I'm just going to depend on you men to tell me what to do."

"Why, I can tell you that right now," Longarm said.

"Just stay where you are and keep a careful watch and shoot before they get a chance to."

"It sounds terribly cold-blooded when you put it that way," Julia said.

"Maybe it does. But I don't guess any of them fellows Don Esquival sent after us would think so, and they're the ones we have to worry about."

As though Longarm's remark had been a cue, a rifle cracked from the brush along the dry river. Above their heads Longarm and Julia heard Clem Brigg's rifle shot as he returned the fire.

Longarm peered out of the gap in the wall. At a point fifty or sixty yards from the corner of the house the brush was quivering. Though Longarm could see no reason for the movement he shouldered his Winchester and sent a slug into the center of the area where he'd seen the branches quivering. A yell of pain from the brushy river below followed his shot. Then a man emerged, limping badly, dragging his rifle behind him.

Longarm had pumped his rifle's loading lever automatically as soon as he'd triggered off his shot. He took quick aim and fired again just as the report of Briggs's weapon cut the air again. The man who'd come out of the brush jerked erect and toppled to the ground, dead.

"You killed him!" Julia exclaimed.

"Better him than us," Longarm replied tersely without moving his eyes off his rifle sights as he worked the loading lever. "Maybe I dropped him, maybe Clem did. But there's another one down there that ain't going to be shooting at us."

He saw the brush beyond the fallen man moving and raised his sights to follow the quivering of the tall bushes and small trees. He'd found no target when Clem

Briggs's weapon barked again, and from the way the brush shook his shot had put another of their attackers out of action.

"We're hurting them a lot worse'n they're hurting us," he said to Julia. "I never did get a good count of how many of them fellows there were in that bunch, but that makes three less than there were when they started out."

"I didn't look back very often while we were trying to get away from them," Julia said, "but I'd guess there were six or seven."

"Either way you count, we've put down about half of 'em, then," Longarm said thoughtfully. "Which sure drops the odds down quite considerable."

Longarm had not taken his eyes off the strip of brush while he and Julia were talking. He saw a sudden shaking and swaying in the head-high vegetation and brought up his rifle again. He held it shouldered and waited, his eyes fixed on the area where the brush had first been disturbed.

Before he could squeeze off the shot he'd planned he saw that the tops of the high growth were now swaying in two areas. Choosing the closest, he fired a blind shot into it, then as quickly as he could lever another shell into the Winchester's chamber he took quick aim at the second area where the brush was trembling and let off a second shot.

A rifle barked from above, where Briggs was stationed. Now there was no further movement in the belt of high growth between the house and the open stretch beyond the brush.

Several long minutes ticked away before Julia broke the silence. "They're awfully quiet now. Do you think they're gone?"

129

"That's hard to say, Julia, but my guess is that it ain't likely," Longarm replied. He gestured toward the high line of growth as he went on, "I can still see one of them fellows that me or Clem brought down. He ain't moved, so I guess he's dead. It ain't likely the others'd go without taking his body with 'em. All we can do is wait and see what they do next."

As though his words had been a cue, a rifle muzzle with a rag of white tied to it rose above the line of brush and scrubby trees that the attackers had used to cover their movements.

"Look!" Julia exclaimed. "They're signaling that they want to surrender!"

"Maybe and maybe not," Longarm said without moving his eyes off the improvised flag. "Might be they just want to talk."

"Are you going to talk to them?"

"Oh, sure. I just hope I know enough of their lingo, or one of them knows enough English so's we can."

"Well, I'm not what you'd call fluent in Spanish, but if you need some help—"

"Sure," Longarm agreed. "But I'll try something I can savvy first." Raising his voice, he called, "That white flag mean you men want to give up?"

Without emerging from the cover of the brush that concealed him, the flag waver replied, "This we do not say! We will talk first, no?"

"Go ahead and say your piece. We're listening," Longarm called back.

"You must surrender to us! If you do not, we will kill you!"

"If that's all you got to say, you can quit right now!" Longarm replied. "And we know how many men you got left! Now, you've said your piece and I've said mine. I'll give you just two minutes to get outa here, or we'll start shooting again, and you'll likely get the first bullet, because I got my sights dead on you!''

"Do not shoot!" the hidden man replied almost before Longarm had finished speaking. "We do only what our *patròn* say we must!"

"All right, you had your say!" Longarm called back. "And you've heard mine! We know how many of you is left, and we don't scare worth a tinker's damn! We'll give you two minutes to pick up them dead men outa your bunch and start back to where you came from! If you ain't on your way by then, we'll start shooting again!"

This time the silence from the strip of bushes lasted even longer than before. Longarm lifted his rifle as though he was about to shoulder it, and his move brought an immediate reaction. The hidden man shouted again, and this time there was no mistaking the sincerity in his voice.

"This thing we will do!" he called. "But say again that you will not shoot at us as we go away!"

"You got my word on that," Longarm answered. "Now, start moving! You got two minutes, like I said! If you ain't all heading out by then, all bets are off!"

Chapter 11

Longarm, Clem and Julia stood silently in the gaping glassless window opening of the big room's front wall, watching the remnants of Don Esquival's defeated gunfighters who still remained alive. The men who'd ridden up with such confidence to attack them were retreating, moving slowly in straggled disarray across the prairie on their way back to the new headquarters of the Hinojosa ranch. The little group was a sorry contrast to what it had been when the attack started. It was obvious that the defeat they'd suffered had cut deeply into their arrogance and pride as well as into their number.

Only three of the six men who'd formed the original group sent to attack the abandoned hacienda were now riding erect in their saddles. Their shoulders drooped, their heads hung down, and they were letting their horses plod listlessly instead of whipping them into a gallop. The lifeless bodies of the other three men Don Esquival had sent were draped across the backs of their mounts.

"They don't look near as mean and feisty as they did when we were watching 'em ride up here," Longarm commented without taking his eyes off the retreating horsemen.

"No, they don't," Clem Briggs agreed. "And I don't suppose they're really the ones who ought to've taken the beating. Now, if we were looking at old Don Esquival Hinojosa instead of his hired hands, I wouldn't feel a bit sorry for him, like I halfway do for those poor whipped devils out there."

"I suppose you're right," Julia said slowly. "But the one I really do feel sorry for is Don Esquival's poor little granddaughter."

"Now, that don't make much sense," Longarm said. "She didn't have any part of sending them fellows after us. Chances are she don't even know right now what her granddaddy did."

"Oh, I'm sure you're right," Julia said. "But when I think about the kind of life she must lead, under Don Esquival's thumb all the time, knowing nothing about the kind of man her grandfather really is—well, she's got some very rude shocks ahead of her."

"I don't suppose your sympathy's misplaced," Briggs said. "Since you spent enough time with her for the two of you to get fairly well acquainted."

"Not really," Julia told him. "We weren't together long enough. Carmelita began telling me about her painting and drawing, but we were just beginning to talk about it when Don Esquival ordered us to get out of his house. I didn't even have time to thank her properly for the map of the ranch that she gave me."

"I recall you saying she gave you something, but I

wasn't paying all that much mind when you were telling us. Why'd she give you anything?'' Longarm asked. "You just said you hadn't had much time to visit.''

"Surely you know the old Spanish custom these people brought here with them, Longarm,'' Julia replied.

"I might, but right now I don't remember,'' Longarm said.

"If your memory needs refreshing, when a guest in a Spanish home admires something, almost anything, the host insists on giving it to them, no matter how valuable it is.''

"Well, a piece of paper with some scribbles on it wouldn't be such a much of a present,'' Longarm said.

"I thought it was,'' Julia told him a bit tartly. "Why, Carmelita must've spent hours on drawing that map she gave me. I could see she was really proud of it, and when I complimented her on it she immediately insisted on giving it to me. She even wrapped it up in an older map so it wouldn't get creased or soiled.''

"So you got two maps instead of one,'' Longarm said. "And I don't guess—'' He stopped short, a frown forming on his face. After a moment of thoughtful silence he went on, "Wait a minute. Why'd old Don Esquival need a new map of his place? Him and his family's had their land for a real long spell, maybe as much as two hundred years. I'd bet dollars to doughnuts that there're maps of their ranch in the land office in Santa Fe and likely in the land office branch in Taos.''

"Carmelita didn't say why her grandfather had the new maps made,'' Julia answered. "But she mentioned that he has some artist come to the ranch every year or so and draw new ones. I guess the maps must get soiled by being handled, or they fade, or something like that.''

Longarm said nothing for a moment, lighting a fresh cigar and puffing it to bring it to full life. When its tip was glowing evenly he took the cigar from his mouth and said, "Clem, I'm starting to get a sorta idea what this ruckus here's all about. Suppose you tell me if I'm wrong."

"Wrong about what?" Briggs asked.

"Don't hurry me, now," Longarm replied. He was silent for a moment while puffing his cigar, then he took the glowing cheroot from his mouth and went on, "Clem, how much do you know about the land laws here in the territory? Before it was United States land, I mean."

"Not a whole lot, because the marshal's office doesn't have a great deal to do with land laws," Briggs answered promptly. "I know they're a little bit different from the laws in the States, because I've heard Frank Maltby—he's the land office chief in Santa Fe—complain about them."

"You're saying he came to you for help?" Longarm looked puzzled as he asked the question.

"I don't suppose you'd run into that sort of job in Denver, because some parts of the laws in the States are different from the ones here in New Mexico Territory," Briggs said. "Once in a while when I was still chief marshal, Maltby would come to me to have our men serve papers on some land grabbers."

"Now, I imagine when you say 'land grabbers' you mean folks that're squatting on land that belongs to somebody else, or maybe to the government?" Longarm asked.

"That's right. Squatters who were trying to claim some land that belonged to the original settlers. But I still don't see what you're getting at, Longarm."

136

"Just pull your reins tight a minute and be quiet while I do a little bit of looking," Longarm told him. Turning to Julia, he went on, "I guess you got them maps that Don Esquival's granddaughter gave you?"

"Of course," Julia replied. "They're in my saddle-bags over there in the corner."

"You mind getting 'em, Julia? I'd like to take a look at 'em, if you don't object."

"Of course I don't." Julia crossed over to her sad-dlebags and took out the rolled drawings. When she returned and handed the roll to Longarm she went on, "This roll got a few dents in it when I tucked it in my saddlebag, but I'm sure they'll straighten out."

Longarm was working the twine off the paper cylinder as Julia spoke. When he'd unrolled the drawings he tried to hold one spread out in each of his hands, but the thick, stiff paper persisted in rerolling itself in spite of his ef-forts. After struggling for a moment he turned to Julia.

"Reckon I'll need a little bit of help if I aim to look at these," he said as he handed one of the sheets of oversized drawing paper to Julia and the other to Briggs. "Maybe if you hold on to one and Clem holds the other one, I can see 'em both at the same time. Just hold 'em alongside each other while I do a mite of looking."

"I still don't know what you're looking for, or why you're even interested in them," Julia said.

"Like I said a minute ago, I'm playing a hunch," Longarm told her. "Now, if you and Clem will just stay quiet for a minute, I'll see how good it is."

Standing in front of Julia and Clem, Longarm bent forward and studied the two drawings for what seemed to the holders to be a long time. At last he straightened up and nodded.

"Well, now," he said. "Them maps get to be real interesting when you study 'em a little while."

"I still don't understand why these drawings interest you so much," Julia said. "Can't you let us in on the reason?"

"Why, sure." Longarm was reaching into his pocket as he spoke. When he drew his hand out it was filled with the ammunition with which he'd filled his pockets before the skirmish with Don Esquival's men began. He went on, "Let's just spread them maps out close together on the floor here, and I'll put some of these cartridges on 'em to keep 'em flat."

For a moment all three of them were busy carrying out Longarm's request. When the maps were spread side by side on the floor and the curling edges of the big sheets of thick drawing paper were held flat by rifle bullets, they showed a remarkable similarity and at the same time were subtly different.

Longarm hunkered down beside the outspread maps and his companions were quick to follow his example.

"Now, look here," Longarm began, putting a finger on the outline of one of the drawings. "I figure what we got is a way that old Don Esquival uses them to keep track of where his critters oughta be put to graze at different times. It's been a long stretch of years back, but when I was a young buck starting out to wrangle cattle on ranches I saw a map a lot like these, and I still remember it pretty good. The boss used it to show his herders and range riders where he wanted the cattle put."

"And the colors represent the good and bad grazing areas," Julia put in. "Of course. It would make his job a lot easier."

"I've never been a cowhand," Briggs said, "but

138

something like this is certainly easy to understand.''

They fell silent as they studied the maps. Blocked-in squares and rectangles that represented the main buildings of the Hinojosa home and those of the estate's workers were easily identified. So were the meandering lines colored in blue that traced the courses of the river and its tributary creeks. The big expanses of good grazing land glowed green, the green subtly changing to yellowish green and then fading to a golden yellow that indicated less satisfactory range, while areas that had been left uncolored identified barren soil that held no range worth grazing.

Longarm broke the brief silence that had fallen while they were examining the maps. ''Now, here's what I'm getting at. This new map, the one that old Hinojosa's granddaughter said she drew, it ain't the same as the old one. Look at how much more rangeland it covers.''

''It does at that,'' Briggs agreed, bending forward to get a better look at the outspread maps. ''And now that I've looked at it a while, I've got an idea why.''

''That's about the first thing that struck me,'' Longarm said. ''See here, where this blue line that stands for a river is. It makes a big curve that don't show on the old map. And if you look close you'll see quite a few other places where them creeks and the river don't show the same curves and twists the old map does.''

''Most of the old Spanish royal land grants use rivers to mark property boundaries,'' Briggs said thoughtfully. ''And just like the creeks that flow into it, the Rio Grande and a lot of the other rivers and creeks change their courses every few years.''

Nodding, Longarm went on, ''What strikes me is that this new map old Don Esquival's granddaughter made shows his ranch a lot bigger than the old one does."

"What you're really saying is that the old fellow's been doing some land grabbing," Briggs remarked.

"Exactly," Longarm agreed. "But to hang on to what he steals he'd have to figure out a way to get the new maps into the land office and take out the old ones without anybody tumbling to what was going on."

"Are you thinking the same thing I am?" Briggs asked.

"I'd say it's pretty likely you and me got the same idea at about the same time, Clem," Longarm said. "For Don Esquival to get the switch made he'd have to be paying off somebody in the land office. Somebody that'd be there when there weren't any of the clerks or other help around to see what was going on."

"There's only one man I can think of who'd fit into that job," Briggs said as a thoughtful frown stole over his face. "And that's Frank Maltby. He's the head man, and that makes him about the only one I can think of offhand who can get into the office at any time of the day or night."

Longarm picked up the trail of deduction that both he and Briggs had been following. "But this Maltby fellow doesn't get out of the office much, if he's like most government bosses."

"There's only one federal office in the territory—and I guess most other places—where the head man can move around pretty much as he pleases."

Longarm nodded as he said, "That'd be the chief marshal. I been in quite a few of them offices and Billy Vail's about the only chief I know of that does all his own paperwork. Most of the ones I know about have got a clerk to take care of that."

"Come to think of it, you're right," Briggs agreed. "Whoever's the chief marshal can get out of the office a lot more, too, without having to answer any questions from anybody. Now, being in the land office, Maltby doesn't have as much freedom as Jason Tobin does. Maltby's job is one that he can't get away from, but Tobin could make a little trip to—well, let's say to Pojuaque—without having to do any explaining to anybody."

Julia had been listening to Longarm and her uncle. Now she said, "That would explain why the payoff was made the way it was. Don Esquival sent his man with the money down to Pojuaque and Tobin took it back to Santa Fe and handed it over to Frank Maltby."

"After he'd pulled out a cut for being the go-between," Longarm added. "I'd guess that Don Esquival does his own palm-greasing at the land office branch in Taos."

"Of course," Julia agreed. "Now I can see why Carmelita said the artist her grandfather hired had to spend so much time at their ranch. He was making copies so that the maps in the land office branch in Taos and the main office in Santa Fe would be the same, if anybody compared them."

"Oh, it was a real good swindle," Longarm said. "Old Don Esquival was getting a lot of land without paying for it and saving a big wad of tax money every year to boot. And even a jackass would be able to figure out that Tobin and this Maltby fellow had to be taking a pretty good payoff."

"While Uncle Sam was being cheated out of a lot of money," Briggs added. "You know, Longarm, when I wrote Billy Vail about this thing, I didn't have the least idea that all this was at the bottom of what was going on. I just knew something was wrong, but I couldn't figure out all the whats and whys.''

"Well, it looks like I got half of my job done," Longarm said thoughtfully. "Because this ain't exactly the kind of case a six-gun can settle."

When Longarm fell silent, and a frown of concentration formed on his face, Clem Briggs and Julia watched him for a moment before Briggs said, "I hope you're counting me in on whatever you're planning to do."

"You don't need to worry about that," Longarm assured him. "This ain't the kind of case that's open and shut, like running an escaped convict down and putting him back where he belongs. I can't go shoving into Jason Tobin's office and reading him a charge without a warrant."

"And Tobin would be the only man who can give the final approval for a warrant to be issued," Briggs put in.

"And the other half is that I can't put my handcuffs on a man that holds a job like Tobin does, and haul him off to jail without having the deputies start shooting. And I ain't about to get into a gunfight with men that hold the same job I do. But I guess you've already figured that out."

"Yes," Briggs replied. "I'd imagine that thought occurred to me about the same time it did to you."

"Now, we got one good thing on our side," Longarm went on. "It's a good long stretch of road between here and Santa Fe. There ain't much way I can see for any word about the run-in we had with old Don Esquival's bunch of killers to get to Santa Fe for a couple of days.''

"He might not even think of sending word to Tobin," Briggs suggested.

"Oh, I figure we got a few days to work with," Longarm said. "But that don't mean we got time to shilly-shally around. There's one thing we need to do before we start back, if we get moving on it right away. I was sorta figuring that as long as we're this close to Taos, it'd be a real smart thing to do to go into the land office branch up there and figure out some way of getting a look at the plat map of the land that old Don Esquival's claiming has always been his.''

"You mean the new maps that will show how much land he's not paying taxes on?" Briggs asked.

"Sure," Longarm said. "It seems to me that we're as close to Taos as we're likely to be. Suppose, we just go on over there and take a little look-see.''

"It'd save coming back all the way from Santa Fe," Briggs agreed.

"It'd do more'n that," Longarm went on. "It'd show us whether or not we got this thing all figured out right. If we find one of the new maps of the Hinojosa place in the land office there, it's dollars to doughnuts that there'll be a new one in the Santa Fe office, too.''

"And you wouldn't even have to show your face and maybe spook the local agent, Longarm," Julia put in. "Clem and I have been there before, while we were looking for a place to buy up here in the Rio Arriba. Us going in there wouldn't raise any sort of question about why we stopped in.''

"It'd cost us a day, but it'd be time well spent," Longarm said thoughtfully. "I say we do it. We'll spend the night here and start out at daybreak.''

. . .

Dawn's first pale grey streaks were just beginning to show above the ragged peaks of the Sangre de Cristo Mountains when the three set out from the abandoned hacienda. Now, traveling through country already familiar to Julia and Clem, they moved at a brisk pace. Full daybreak and the rosy sky of the beginning sunrise brought them to a long downslope in the trail, and at its end they could see the scattered blocklike shapes of the houses that made up the tiny village. Most of the small brown adobe houses they passed at the edge of town were still dark, though lights showed in a few of them.

By the time they reached their destination, the sun was peering above the mountaintops and the village itself was beginning to stir. The branch land office was not yet open, but a few people were on the move by the time they rode into the village plaza. A *tortillero* was already at his stand on one side of the plaza, and they dismounted at the edge of the ragged square long enough to supplement their scanty breakfast with some big flour tortillas from his charcoal griddle.

Wiping his chin with the back of his hand to clear away the crumbs of the tortilla he'd just finished, Longarm looked at the awakening plaza and said, "Seems to me that branch land office oughta be open pretty soon, Clem. Since it wouldn't be smart for me to show up at that place, I'm going to see if I can find me a barber, because my whiskers are starting to itch me. You and Julia go on there soon as it opens and take enough time to be sure our hunch about map-switching is right. I'll

144

meet you here on the square when you're done, and we'll cut a shuck for Santa Fe. And once we're there, we won't waste no time in giving Jason Tobin and Frank Maltby their comeuppance.''

Chapter 12

"Even if I'm pretty close to being tuckered out after doing more riding in six days than I usually do in six months, I don't think a single minute of the time we spent in Taos was wasted," Clem Briggs remarked.

"It sure wasn't," Longarm agreed. "You and Julia seeing what you did in the land office branch there proves we were right when we figured out what old Don Esquival's been getting away with. Now just as soon as we get back to Santa Fe we can rest a little while before we take on the rest of our clean-up job."

"While we're talking about resting, is there any reason why we can't stop right here for a few minutes?" Julia asked. "My horse could certainly use a breather, and so could I."

"No reason at all," Longarm answered. "We been pushing pretty hard, and a leg-stretch'd help all of us."

He was reining in as he spoke. For the past half hour

they'd been moving steadily along on one of the few level stretches of the generally uphill road. Far ahead, the rutted path dipped into a shallow valley, and beyond it one last long upgrade marked the crest of the saucerlike depression in which Santa Fe was located.

The exhaustion of the past few strenuous days was beginning to show on all three, and for a few moments after dismounting they did nothing but stamp the ground and kick their feet into the thin air in a sort of impromptu dance to stretch their cramped leg muscles.

Longarm broke the stillness when he said to Clem, "If you and Julia were right about what you found out in the Taos land office branch, we've got old Don Esquival and Tobin and Maltby pushed into a tight corner that they won't be able to get out of."

"Don't worry about anything we told you being mixed up," Briggs assured Longarm. "Neither Julia nor I could be mistaken about a land plat that we've looked at and studied so thoroughly. And I took time to look at the sheet that gives the description of the boundary marks. It was new, too. I'll swear to that in court."

"There wasn't a bit of doubt about it," Julia put in. "Clem insisted on taking Mr. Fuentes—the land office agent—to get a drink at the little saloon next door, and that left me free to do just about anything I wanted to. I knew where the file for Don Esquival's land is kept because the agent had shown it to us before."

"You never mentioned that to me, Julia," Longarm said.

"Because I'd forgotten seeing it," she replied. "And I'm sure Clem had, too. It was only a glimpse and the page was upside down."

"Of course, neither one of us realized what we were

148

looking at," Clem put in. "All we were thinking about then was buying the old hacienda."

"I saw just enough of the old map to be sure the new one had already been substituted for the one we saw before," Julia said.

"I'd say that pretty well settles it, then," Longarm said. "And if the map up at Taos has been switched, it'd stand to reason the one in Santa Fe's been changed, too."

"And Julia and I were both careful not to give away what we were really looking for," Briggs said.

"Then all we got to do when we get to Santa Fe is make sure the new map and boundary sheets have been switched, and that won't be hard to do," Longarm said, as much to himself as to his companions. "And then comes the hard part."

"Proof?" Briggs asked. "Enough evidence to connect Jason Tobin and Frank Maltby to the case?"

Longarm nodded. "All of us know who's mixed up in this swindle, but it might not be easy to get a judge to see things the way we do. There ain't much need to fret about that now, though. We got a good spell of riding ahead, and we'll have plenty of time to figure out how we can go about proving what we know's been going on, so don't let's jump off that bridge till we come to it."

"It looks like we'll be getting into Santa Fe just before night hits," Longarm remarked. "And a few minutes one way or the other ain't going to make all that much difference. Let's give the horses one last breather when we get to the top of this uphill drag."

"I'd say we're due for a breather ourselves," Clem agreed.

Julia, riding between the two men, murmured a wordless throaty second to the suggestion.

Dusk was shading to darkness as they reached the top of the lengthy upslope ride and reined in. The crest was marked by a ragged line of chest-high boulders that stretched from the road along the rim on both sides. They did not bother to pull off the rutted thoroughfare, but left their horses standing in the gap while they stood beside the animals and stamped their feet and stretched.

Although to the west and overhead the cloudless sky was still a light blue, long shadows that signaled the sudden onset of night at that mile-high altitude were creeping across the terrain at the end of the long downgrade ahead. Darkness was veiling the bottom of the shallow, saucerlike depression in which Santa Fe stood, and in the town's houses a few lights were already beginning to show.

"It'll be full dark by the time we get into town," Clem Briggs observed. "I don't suppose there'll be much we can do with what little bit's left of the day."

"Not likely," Longarm agreed.

"And maybe that's just as well," Julia put in. "Clem, I can see how tired you are after all the riding we've done, on top of that fight with Don Esquival's men. You need to rest."

"Don't worry about me, I'll make out fine the rest of the way," Briggs assured her. "It's not too much farther, and all of it's downhill."

"We ain't none of us daisy fresh," Longarm commented. "But we're so close now the rest of the way

150

ain't going to be so bad. All we got left to do is push on into town, then we can call it a day.''

They remounted and twitched on their horses' reins, and the weary animals began plodding down the long slope ahead. As they dropped below the rim of the depression the darkness seemed to move forward to meet them, and the number of lights that had been visible only a few minutes earlier were multiplying rapidly.

Ahead the road narrowed where it passed through a gap between two high sandstone bluffs. To let Clem and Julia enter the narrow passage Longarm took the slack out of the reins without breaking his horse's stride. Clem vanished into the strip of deepening gloom between the sides of the high rock formation and Julia followed.

Longarm was just entering the shadowed gap that broke the high-rising sides when the first shot cut through the evening's silence. It was followed quickly by two or more. Longarm dug his heels into his mount's flanks and the animal leaped ahead. As he emerged from the passageway Longarm saw Clem's riderless horse rearing beside the narrow road, and as he flicked his eyes rapidly over the terrain ahead he saw Julia dismounting. There was no sign of Clem.

In the short interval of no more than a few seconds that separated the first shot and the third, Longarm had pulled his Winchester from its saddle scabbard. By habit he'd swept his eyes across the terrain ahead while he was drawing and shouldering the rifle. Another shot broke the stillness and a spurt of red muzzleblast ahead gave him a target. He fired and a yell of pain came with the dying crack of the rifle.

Another blaze of crimson muzzleblast flashed in the low growing *chamisal* that bordered the narrow road.

The red spurt gave Longarm a new target. He swung the muzzle of his rifle and loosed a shot in reply. There was no shout of pain, but the tops of the brush began trembling. Realizing that he'd missed and that the man who'd done the shooting was escaping, Longarm pumped two more slugs into the moving shrubs.

He did not wait to see the effects of his blind shooting, for as he got off his second round a rifle barked from the opposite side of the narrow road and its lead whistled uncomfortably close to his face. Swiveling in his saddle, Longarm answered the shot with one of his own. He had no target, and no answering round came from the rifleman who'd initiated the attack.

Knowing that he now had only two more rounds left in his rifle's chamber, Longarm rested his Winchester across his knees and drew his Colt. He was waiting for the next shot from the brush and his wait was a short one. Muzzleblast stabbed the steadily deepening dusk from the side of the road where he'd seen the first red spurt, but now he was ready. Swinging his Colt in a smooth arc, Longarm loosed three shots in quick succession, and a gargled yell of pain followed.

In the near distance, off the road where the *chamisal* grew high and thick, a man called, "Let's get the hell outa here! We got one, we can tend to the others later!"

Though he had little faith in voice shots, the success of his first two blind rounds encouraged Longarm to send one of his two remaining rifle bullets into the area from which the voice had come. This time no yell followed and the sharp thunking of hoofbeats sounded. The rider quickly reached the end of the shielding *chamisal*, and Longarm found his target, the black form of the

152

retreating rider outlined against the deepened blue of the sky.

Aiming quickly, Longarm fired the last round in his rifle's chamber. He could not be sure that the shot he triggered off had been effective, for in the instant before his Winchester cracked the fleeing rider jerked his reins and started the horse veering onto the downslope. A glance told Longarm that the man was beyond his Colt's effective range.

By this time the hoofbeats of the horse ridden by the bushwhacker on the opposite side of the road were so faint that they were almost inaudible. The eastern sky had already taken on the deep hue of full night, and Longarm realized at once that even if he'd had a fully loaded rifle he could empty it into the gloom without any real hope of success.

As he started to reload his Winchester, Julia's call reached him through the darkness. "Longarm! I need your help! Clem's been hit!"

Longarm wasted no time. He did not stop to reload, but moved at once in the direction of Julia's voice. He crossed the road at the base of its flanking cliffs and peered through the gloom trying to locate her. The darkness was almost total now, but when Longarm bent forward he could see the disturbed waving of the tops of the thick *chamisal* that marked her position, and a dozen long quick steps took him to her side. Now he could also see Clem stretched on the ground beside her.

"Thank goodness!" she said. "I was afraid you wouldn't be able to find me, it got so dark so fast."

"How bad's he hurt?" Longarm asked.

Before Julia could answer, Clem spoke for himself. "Not as bad as Julia thinks," he replied. "The bastard put a slug into my shoulder, but I don't think it hit a bone."

Digging a match from his pocket, Longarm flicked his thumbnail across its head. He closed his eyes before the match sputtered into its first bright glare of flame and opened them slowly, giving his eyes time to adjust to the small pool of brightness shed by the burning match.

In the brief time before the match burned out he saw that Clem was stretched on the ground, propped on one elbow. Julia knelt behind him, her bloodstained hands clamped around her uncle's armpit.

"I think I've stopped the bleeding," she said, looking at her hands. "But I'm afraid to let go now."

"Just hold on to him a minute," Longarm instructed her. "I got to get out my bandana. It'll just have to do for a little while, till we can get into town and find a doctor."

"Let's try Fort Marcy," Clem said. "The army still keeps a doctor there, and it is a little closer than Santa Fe."

"Sure," Longarm agreed. "But let's take care of that bullet hole before we start to go anyplace."

Longarm had folded his big bandana into a triangle and was now working by feel, rolling it into a long cylinder between his outstretched hands. Then he moved a half-step closer to Julia.

He went on, "Julia, I'm fixing to hunker down there by you now. I'll take hold of Clem and keep him from bleeding soon as you let go. I'm going to put this bandana across my knee where it'll be handy. I don't reckon you carry matches, but you can dig into my coat pocket and you'll feel some. All you got to do is light one off of

154

the other before it goes out while I get him bandaged up to stop him from bleeding.''

"Go ahead," Julia replied promptly. Longarm felt her hand groping in his pocket and then she said, "I've found three or four matches, Longarm. I guess I'm as ready as I'll ever be."

"You might as well go ahead and strike one, then," Longarm told her. "Soon as we switch hands. The minute you let go, I'll grab Clem."

Julia struck a match and held it high. As he fumbled for a moment while he switched holds with her, Longarm got a quick glance at the bullet hole in Clem's shirt. Even against the red stain that spread over much of the fabric, Longarm could see a trickle of blood still oozing from the wound, and he clamped his big hand over the wound as best he could to cover it and keep the flow from continuing any longer.

Julia's match guttered and she touched a fresh one to its dying flame. Longarm was already cinching the rolled bandana into Clem's armpit and drawing its ends together across the top of the wounded shoulder. He pulled them as tight as possible and knotted them, then leaned back to sit on his heels.

"How's it feel?" he asked.

"It's starting to hurt a little bit, but nothing I can't stand," Clem replied.

"You'll be all right," Longarm assured him. "Except you'll have a right sore shoulder for a while."

"That's not going to bother me a bit," Clem replied. "Not when I think what I'd be if that slug had gone a little lower."

"Just the same, we better get you to Fort Marcy," Longarm went on. "It won't take but a minute for them

155

army doctors there to get a real bandage on it.''

"You start toward the road, Longarm," Julia said. "I'll go ahead and get the horses, they're on the other side of the road, down in a little gully."

With Longarm cradling Clem's wounded shoulder as best as he could, they plodded slowly back to the road where Julia was holding the horses. In the saddle again, they set out toward Fort Marcy. They talked little during the remainder of their ride, and as they neared Santa Fe Clem said, "In case you don't know the way to Fort Marcy as well as I do, Longarm, I'll call the turns. We don't go all the way into Santa Fe, just a little ways off to the northeast."

"Sure," Longarm agreed. "If you know some short-cuts, let's take 'em. The sooner a doctor looks at that bullet hole and fixes it up proper, the better."

"You're a lucky man," the army doctor remarked as he tied off the crisscrossed bandage that now covered Clem's shoulder. "If that bullet had gone any higher it would have shattered your collarbone, and if it had gone much lower it would almost certainly have hit your heart or the main artery that feeds it."

"Well, that makes me feel some better," Clem said. "But I'd've been luckier if it had missed me completely."

"What sort of fracas were you in?" the doctor went on. "And exactly where? I'll have to report this to the city police or to the sheriff, depending on where the shooting was."

"You don't have to put yourself out doing that, Doctor," Longarm broke in. He took out his wallet and showed the medico his badge. "I'll take care of them little niggly jobs."

"That'll suit me fine," the doctor said. "But I'll want to keep an eye on my patient until tomorrow evening, at least."

"Now, damn it, that's not necessary!" Clem protested angrily. "I'm perfectly all right!"

He started to get off the operating table where the army doctor had insisted on placing him while putting on the bandage, but his knees buckled and he'd have fallen but for the doctor's quick move and strong supporting arm.

"You better do like the doctor says, Clem," Longarm went on. "Maybe you can't see it, but I sure can from where I'm standing. If that bullet had hit you a couple of inches from where it did, you'd be getting buried instead of bandaged. Now, I'll go on into town with Julia and see that she gets home safe. Then I'll come back out here after you tomorrow."

"Late tomorrow," the doctor put in quickly. "I don't want this man moving around until he's rested and had time to start healing."

"You don't have to worry, Clem," Longarm went on. "Let yourself sorta get over all this. Then we'll finish up that job we got started."

"It doesn't look like I've got much choice," Briggs replied. "But I guess the doctor's right. I'm starting to feel like I need to go to sleep. I'm not going to be much good for anything for a while, I guess."

"You'll feel different about it tomorrow," Longarm assured him. "Now I better go tell Julia you're all right."

When Longarm reached the sallyport he found the sentry who'd blocked Julia from entering Fort Marcy dozing in his coffinlike box, and Julia was pacing back and forth just outside the sallyport.

"How's Clem?" she asked when she saw Longarm. "Is he all right?"

"Right as rain," Longarm assured her. "He ain't going to be cutting up no sort of didoes for a while, but the doctor says that by this time tomorrow he can get up and walk around pretty much like he's used to doing."

"Well, that makes me feel better," she said. "Come on. I had to leave the horses over there at the civilian hitch rail. That fool of a sentry not only wouldn't let me in, he wouldn't even talk to me after you and Clem left."

"Now, you've got all nerved up and upset," Longarm told her as they untied the reins of their mounts from the hitchrail. "I guess you've just been worn to a frazzle, with all the things that's happened these past few days. Come along. I'll ride home with you. I'd imagine you can use some help unsaddling and things like that."

"I'll be perfectly all right," she assured him. "You don't have to baby me, Longarm."

"That's the last thing I'm aiming to do," he replied. "But I sure ain't going to cut away and go crawl in bed and leave you to shift for yourself. Besides, I'm hungry as a she-bear that's just dropped her cubs. There's bound to be a restaurant open this late, even in a little place like Santa Fe. We'll stop off on the way through town and grab a bite to eat, then I'll see you home safe and we'll meet tomorrow and come get Clem when the doctor turns him loose."

"I'll let you see me home on one condition," Julia said. "You come in when we get to Clem's house and I'll fix us a late supper. Don't say no, Longarm, because that's my last word."

Chapter 13

"Would you think I was a careless housekeeper if we just got up and left the table without me clearing our supper dishes away?" Julia asked Longarm. She was smiling mischieviously as she waved her hand to indicate the table where their plates and dishes still remained.

"Why, I wouldn't've noticed it at all if you hadn't mentioned it," Longarm told her. "Eating in restaurants all the time like I do, I ain't used to doing anything but getting up and walking away when I finish a meal. And the grub I fix for myself when I'm working a case outside of a town ain't the kind that's got to be put on a plate."

"Then I'm just going to close this dining-room door and leave everything the way it is," Julia went on. "While we were on that long trip we just took, I found out that you enjoy a cigar after a meal, so let's go sit in the parlor while you smoke one."

Settled down in the parlor, Julia in an easy chair and

Longarm on the divan, he lighted his cigar and drew an appreciative puff or two before he said, "By rights, I oughta be in my hotel room right this minute, figuring out the best way to go about closing this case. But seeing as Clem's the one that got it started, I'd sorta like for him to be in on it all the way to the end. He'll be up and about tomorrow, so I'm going to wait till he can put in his say about things."

"He'll appreciate that, I know," Julia said. "And waiting for him will only put off closing it one day."

"Sure," Longarm agreed. "And I wouldn't feel right if he wasn't in on the windup. And I got all the evidence right now that we'll likely ever get. Us getting jumped this evening on the road so close to Santa Fe can't mean but one thing, Julia."

"That somebody knew we were going to be traveling on it," she broke in quickly.

His face sober, Longarm nodded agreement. He went on, "I figured right away that old Don Esquival had already got word to Jason Tobin that we'd started back here. And something else I figured out is that your little friend Carmelita must've told her granddaddy about giving you that map."

"Now, that hadn't occurred to me," Julia said. "I hope he's not going to punish her for it. I'm sure she didn't realize what a giveaway it'd be."

"She wouldn't've let it out of her hands if she'd known," Longarm said. "And he ain't likely to do much but scold her. She didn't know she was upsetting her grandpa's apple cart."

Julia nodded absently. A thoughtful frown was forming on her face. She said, "He'd have had plenty of time

162

to send word to Jason Briggs that we were on our way back.''

"Oh, sure. I figured from the first that Briggs had to be the one that sent out the bunch that jumped us on the road in.''

"Because we dropped a day behind, taking that trip to Taos,'' Julia added. "It was well worthwhile, though.''

"Oh, I'll grant you that. So maybe it's just a sorta swap, only we come out of it ahead.''

"How do you mean, Longarm?''

"Why, everything that's happened is going to help our case when it gets in front of a judge,'' he replied. "Now that we know where to look, it'll be easy to dig up all the evidence we need to prove that Don Esquival's been paying off Tobin and Maltby to cheat the government. Judges have got hard heads, Julia. They don't want a bunch of ifs and maybes. They want proof.''

Longarm had barely finished speaking when the little clock on the mantle began chiming. Both he and Julia looked at it, and before it had reached its eleventh and final chime Longarm was getting to his feet.

"Time sorta got away from us,'' he said. "I got to be moving along, Julia.''

"Why should you go?'' Julia asked. "It's not that I'm nervous or afraid, but those men who tried to kill us on the road must know where I live.''

"There ain't no question about that. They probably know where I'm staying, too.''

"Oh, they're not stupid,'' Julia agreed. "With Jason Tobin on their side they'll certainly know by now where to find us, and I'm sure nothing's going to stop them from making another try.''

163

"If I was in their shoes, that's what I'd do," Longarm said. "They know I have to be staying at a hotel, and there ain't all that many hotels in Santa Fe. It'd be easy enough for them to find the one I'm at."

"There's an easy way to keep them from bothering you, Longarm. I don't think they'd expect you to be here with me."

Longarm kept his face from showing his surprise as he asked, "You mean you're asking me to stay the night?"

"I don't see why you shouldn't, if you don't object to sleeping in Clem's bed. I know I'd feel a lot better if you were here instead of at the hotel, and I'm sure we'd both be safer."

"When you put it that way, I guess I got to agree with you," Longarm said thoughtfully. "It makes sense that them bushwhackers that got away from us on the road ain't going to give up trying, and they can move at night a lot easier than in broad open daylight."

"If you're going to stay here, you'd better put your horse in the barn with mine and Clem's, then," Julia suggested. "Just lead him back along the left side of the house."

"I don't imagine I'll have any trouble finding it."

Julia went on, "I made up both Clem's bedroom and mine before we started for the Rio Arriba country so they'd be ready for us when we got back and I wouldn't have to fuss around with them when I was tired."

"Sure," Longarm said. "Now, it's going to take me a few minutes to put the horse in the barn and take his saddle off. Why don't you just show me right now where Clem's room is. We'll say our goodnights, and then I won't have to bother you when I come back in."

164

• • •

Accustomed as he was to sleeping in strange beds and relaxed following his hot bath, Longarm had dropped off to sleep only a few minutes after pulling the blanket over his shoulders to keep out the chill of mile-high Santa Fe's night air. When sleeping in a strange bed he was also accustomed to awakening fully alert and reaching for the Colt that he always placed beside his pillow if even the smallest noise reached his ears.

A faint rasping of metal rubbing metal from the door across the room had been enough to rouse him. The rays of the late-rising full moon trickling around the windowshade gave the room a dim ghostly light, and Longarm was sitting up in bed with his revolver leveled at the doorway when it swung open.

Framed against the rectangle of the door Julia was standing, the light hue of her floor-length nightgown giving her the appearance of a ghostly figure from some child's fairy tale.

"Goodness, Longarm!" she gasped when light from the opened door flooded Longarm's room and she saw the muzzle of the Colt unwaveringly pointing at her. "I thought you'd be sound asleep by now."

"I was," he replied. "But I sleep with my ears wide open. What's wrong, Julia?"

"Nothing, unless it's me."

"After the way you were talking a little while back, it don't sound to me like there's much wrong except that you don't want to be by yourself," he commented. "There ain't a thing wrong with you that I can see. Did you hear a noise or something?"

"No. And I was so tired from our trip and so relaxed after my bath that I thought I'd sleep like a log. I did doze for a little while, then I got to thinking about you being in here, and wondering if you felt as alone as I did. The longer I thought, the more I wondered and the wider awake I got, so I decided to come and find out.''

"You want me to get up and light a lamp so we can visit?''

"I'm sure you know quite well why I came in here,'' Julia replied. "By the time we finished supper, I was convinced that you weren't going to be the one who'd make an advance.''

"You sound like you were just waiting for me to get pushy.''

"Longarm, I'm a grown woman, not just Clem's little niece.''

"That's sure easy to see, you standing there in that flimsy nightgown. Oh, you're a grown woman, all right, Julia. And a real pretty one, too.''

"I thought you'd never get around to saying so. Now stop being polite and move over. I've been without a man too long, and you're the first one I've seen in a long time that I feel like going to bed with.''

As she spoke, Julia was moving into the room. Longarm's groin began twitching in the beginning of an erection as he watched her drop the filmy nightgown from her shoulders. Julia did not stop, but continued her deliberate progress toward the bed. Now Longarm could see quite clearly the rosy bosom spots of her full upthrust breasts and the darker patch of her pubic triangle.

"You know you're welcome,'' he said.

"I didn't expect you to send me back to my own bed,'' she answered as she settled down beside him.

"And I wasn't looking for you to come in here with me. But I'm sure glad you did.''

As Longarm spoke he was sliding his arm around Julia's waist. She turned to him, her head thrown back, and he took her unspoken invitation by pressing his lips to hers. Julia's warm tongue slid to meet his. They held their first kiss while her soft hands stroked Longarm's chest, then strayed down his sides to find his crotch and begin a gentle fondling of his full erection with her fingertips.

"You're big," Julia whispered as she turned her head slowly to break their kiss. "Almost from the first minute I saw you I've been wondering if you might be. I'm glad, because I like big men."

"Well, then I'm glad too," Longarm told her. "Now, you say when you're ready, and do what pleases you the most."

"I'm ready now, but I know it'll be better later, so let's not be too impatient," she said softly. "It'll be better if we wait a little bit. I've been without a man so long that I want to enjoy just being so close to you and felling you for a while first."

"Sure. And I ain't in all that big a hurry. I reckon I feel about the same way you do."

Longarm slid his hand from Julia's waist up to the firm globes that now invited his attention. For a moment or two he rubbed them softly, then he started caressing the stiffened tips of her budded rosettes with his fingertips. Julia's body began twitching now. She threw one leg over Longarm's hips and crouched above him, then leaned forward to find his lips with hers once more.

Their lips met and after a moment Julia's tongue crept out. She thrust it into his mouth and their tongues entwined, prodding and seeking. Her body was twitching now, and Longarm grasped her waist between his hands to support her while she rotated her hips, rubbing against his rigid shaft. She moved faster and faster, then broke their prolonged kiss to throw her head back and gasp while the gyrations of her hips grew more and more frantic.

Lifting her head, she breathed softly, "I can't wait any longer to feel you inside me!"

Even before she'd finished speaking, Julia dropped her hips to impale herself, but Longarm slid his hands down her sides and grasped them in time to stop her from achieving a full penetration.

"No!" she protested. "I want you in me all the way!"

"Just hold back for a bit," he suggested. "Go on like you were doing. I liked that as much as you did."

Julia was gasping now. She began rotating her hips, still pressing heavily on Longarm's hands as she tried to push down and complete the penetration she'd begun. Even as she began her effort her body began trembling and a cry of joy bubbled from her lips. Longarm held her firmly while her buttocks jerked and her body quivered, gently at first, then spastically.

Her wild gyrations went on for only a few moments before they started to fade. She sagged and sighed and said, "Damn it, Longarm! You got me started and then wouldn't help me finish!"

"Don't think about that," he replied. "Just hold still for a minute and you'll forget all about it."

Without breaking the bond of flesh that connected them, Longarm began turning them on the bed. Julia grasped his intention at once. Locking her arms around his back she held herself rigid while he moved. After a few moments she sank back on the bed and he released her. She relaxed the pressure of her legs against his hips and spread her thighs wide.

"Oh, yes," she whispered. "Now I'm more than ready!"

"Me, too," Longarm agreed.

He drove hard then, a quick short lunge that brought a cry of ecstasy from Julia. Somehow Julia managed to spread her thighs even wider than they'd been when she was straddling him. Longarm recognized her invitation. He finished his partial penetration by driving into her, lunging in a sudden thrust that brought their bodies together with a soft sound of flesh meeting flesh and also brought a shuddering cry of ecstasy from Julia's throat.

Even now Longarm did not begin driving at once. He held himself firmly against Julia's warm quivering body for several moments while the shudders that were sweeping through her body rippled and faded and came to an end. She lay quiescent for only a moment, then began to rotate her hips. She moved slowly at first, but after a few moments she speeded up her gyrations, twisting her hips as she moved.

Longarm held himself against her soft warm flesh for a short time before starting to stroke, slowly and deliberately. Julia began sighing, a low throaty bubbling sound that lasted for only a few moments at a time. When Longarm sped up the rhythm of his lunges her sighs grew sharper and spilled from her lips at shorter and shorter intervals. He paced himself to keep up his regular deliberate tempo until Julia's breathy sighs were no longer broken by short intervals of silence, but flowed from her throat in a steady stream.

Julia began trembling and the measured rocking of her hips in response to Longarm's lunges gave way to a constant rocking while the trembling shudders that had been sweeping through her body were no longer interrupted. Longarm drove lustily now, with deep thrusts that brought small shrieks of joy from Julia's quivering lips. Her body was quaking now, her hips rocking, her legs locked tightly around Longarm's back.

He was ready for Julia's final signals, loud cries that broke from her throat at shorter and shorter intervals until they exploded into a constant throaty keening. Her hips gyrated uncontrollably and her legs grew taut as she tried to pull his driving shaft into her even more deeply.

Julia was quivering now. Her shudders had speeded into a series of sweeping waves that shook her entire body. Her hips were twisting wildly, her heels kept drumming on Longarm's back. Her cries had merged into a constant column of ecstatic sound, her head was pressing back deeply into her pillow and her eyes were closed, their lids pressed tightly together.

Longarm was not far behind her. His driving thrusts became more powerful as well as growing erratic in the moments before his own climax took him. Julia's pleasure was cresting now, and with a final lusty lunge he buried his rigid shaft and held himself pressed firmly to her soft and still-quivering body as he jetted and trembled to his long-delayed climax while beneath him Julia's warm softness cushioned his fading spasm.

Neither of them spoke, and after a few moments the exhaustion that followed their fervent embrace began to fade. Julia was the first to move. Her arms had been locked around Longarm's shoulders during the final moments of their shared ecstasy, and now she let them fall beside her. Then Longarm moved, breaking the bond of flesh.

170

"I hope you feel as good as I do, Longarm," Julia said softly. "I've got to admit, I thought about it and hesitated for a long time before I came in here."

"I reckon you were in the same fix I was," he replied. "But I figured it wasn't something I oughta do, go pushing into your room, much as I felt like it."

"I'm sure you know now that you'd certainly have been welcome. At first I had an idea about calling you to come in, but then I decided that the best thing to do was to—well, to do as I did. But I'd better go back to my own bed now. Both of us need some sleep after the busy day we've had."

"I don't know about you," Longarm told Julia, "but I still feel fresh as a daisy. Let's just stay right where we are. We have to do some planning about tomorrow, and this is as good a time as any to take care of that. And when we've settled it, I have some different ideas about—well, we'll talk about them when the right time comes."

Looking at Julia across the table that still held the plates and coffee cups of their belated breakfast, Longarm asked, "You're sure you got rested up enough to go ahead?"

"I feel better than I have for weeks. Don't worry, Longarm. I'll be just fine."

"You're certain you've got it all straight?"

"I'm positive," she assured him.

"Then I don't guess there's anything left to do but go get started. I saddled Clem's horse, and we'll lead it with us, because from what that doctor said last night he'll be ready to come back with us. The horses are as ready as you and me, and we're as ready as we'll ever be."

Cerillos Road was almost deserted at that hour of the morning. The Santa Feans who lived in the modest adobe houses that straggled along the narrow rock-strewn thoroughfare had long ago departed for their jobs. Longarm and Julia crossed the plaza with only a quick glance at the rambling adobe building that housed the marshal's office and turned to follow Palace Avenue to the rutted road that led them to Fort Marcy.

Chapter 14

There was no sentry at the sallyport this time, and after a quick exchange of glances Julia continued to ride beside Longarm until they pulled rein at the infirmary. Clem Briggs was the first person they saw when they stepped inside. He was dressed in the clothes he'd worn the day before and was pacing restlessly up and down the wide corridor. His back was toward them and he did not see Longarm and Julia until she called to him. Then he whirled and hurried to meet them. He started talking in a loud angry voice even before he reached them.

"What held you up so long?" he asked. "These damn fools woke me up before daylight for an examination. The doctor gave me a quick look and said I was all right, that I could go home."

"And we've come to get you, so that's where we'll go," Julia said placatingly. "Just as soon as you're ready."

"Ready?" Briggs was obviously angry. "I've been ready ever since that doctor told me I was all right. Then when I asked if I could borrow a remount horse to ride home they said it was against some new rule they've got. I asked if I could have a bite of breakfast while I waited for you and Longarm, but they said that was against the rules, too."

"You must be starved!" Julia broke in. "What kind of an infirmary is this, where they make patients go hungry?"

"Army red tape," Briggs snapped. Then, as his temper began to return to normal, he went on, "It seems I'd been discharged as soon as that examination was over and wasn't a patient any longer or a soldier on active duty!"

"Now, simmer down, Clem," Longarm said soothingly. "You had a bad night, I reckon, but that's over and done with."

"I guess I just had to take my mad out on somebody," Briggs said. "I've been waiting for you ever since, and I just got mad as hell and hungry, too. And I didn't have any right to give you two the rough edge of my tongue. It wasn't your fault."

"Just forget all about it," Julia told him. "Longarm and I understand."

"Sure," Longarm agreed. Frowning then, he went on, "I want to have a quick word with that doctor who fixed you up. Just stay here for a minute and talk to Julia, and I'll be back in no time."

After Longarm had started away, Briggs turned back to Julia. "What did you two find out after you left me here?"

"By the time we got into town, it was too late to find

174

out much of anything," she explained. "We talked a while, and went to bed. I'm sure Longarm's got some sort of plan now, because he said something about me going to the land office later on, and he's going to the marshal's office. But he may want to change his plans, now that we're sure you're all right."

"I'm as all right as I'll ever be," Briggs grumbled. "And just as anxious as I was yesterday to see that crook Tobin and his bunch behind bars where they belong. The sooner—"

Briggs broke off as Longarm came through the door, and with Julia following started to meet him. Longarm nodded assuringly and gestured for them to join him.

"They said you're fit to travel, Clem. And the doctorings on the house since you were once a federal marshal."

"Then let's get started," Clem said impatiently. "I won't feel right until I get some breakfast inside me. While I eat, you can tell me what sort of scheme you've cooked up."

"So that's how me and Julia figured to work it," Longarm concluded. He and Julia and Briggs were sitting around the table in Briggs's home. Briggs had just finished his long-delayed breakfast and was pushing his plate away.

Longarm went on, "All Julia's supposed to do is keep that Maltby fellow at the land office busy till I get there. She can do that easy enough, but it'll be better if you go along with her, just in case something goes wrong. I'll take care of Jason Tobin and his crooked deputies without no trouble."

Briggs was silent for a moment before saying, "That's

not good odds you'll be bucking, Longarm. I agree with you about Maltby and the land office, he won't even know what's up. But Briggs and his bunch, that's something else. For openers, you'll have three deputies besides Tobin to handle."

"Just two," Longarm said. "I don't figure that young Espinosa fellow's going to mix into it. If he was on Tobin's side he wouldn't't've come to the hotel and tipped me off about Maltby and Tobin the other night."

"Then that just leaves three."

"Well, now, Clem, I ain't aiming to brag none, but Jason Tobin and his two renegades are going to be bottled up in that long narrow room, and I can handle them by myself without no trouble."

"If you're leaving me out because you think I'm hurt too badly to handle a gun, you're wrong," Briggs said, shaking his head. "I don't have any authority to tell you what to do, but you can deputize me if you feel like it. If you don't, I'll just have to . . ."

"Do what?" Longarm asked when Briggs paused.

"I don't quite know," Briggs admitted.

"Will you two stop squabbling?" Julia broke in. "Longarm, I think you're the one who ought to give in. If I know Clem at all, he was about to say he'd tag down to the marshal's office anyhow, and I wouldn't put it past him to do it."

"Julia's right, you know," Briggs said.

"I guess I know when I better change my mind," Longarm said. "I'd feel like you do, Clem, if I were in your place. And I'll be glad to have you on my side."

"You'd've had a hell of a time stopping me." Briggs's smile matched Longarm's. He went on, "Now, I've got an idea or two of my own, if you'd like to hear them."

"Sure. Trot 'em out."

"Well, I know that office better than you do," Briggs went on. "And we'll be up against three men."

"Three ain't such a much to handle," Longarm told him again. "And they ain't looking for us to bust in. But if we both go in by the front door, we're just one target. I ain't much one for iffing, but if there was just a back-door to that—"

"There is," Briggs broke in.

"If there's a back door there, I never did see it," Longarm said.

"You wouldn't. It's behind the chief marshal's cubbyhole, hard to see unless you're looking for it or unless you know it's there. But it'd be an easy bolt-hole for Tobin."

"And he'd be the kind that'd use it, too," Longarm said. He was thoughtfully silent for a moment, then went on, "I'd say we better do some plan-switching. Have you got any druthers?"

"I know the layout of the place better than you do. If you'll take the front, I'll go in the back."

"Fair enough," Longarm said. "And there ain't no use in shilly-shallying around. The sooner we get on the job the quicker it'll be finished."

As Longarm and Briggs reined their horses over to the hitch rail outside the U.S marshal's office, the former chief marshal remarked, "I guess what you're thinking runs pretty much along the same lines as what I am, Longarm."

"You mean going up against men that're wearing the same badge we do?"

"Something like that."

177

"Sure. I've given it some thought these last few minutes," Longarm admitted. "And I don't mind saying it don't make me feel real good."

"Or me," Briggs agreed.

"Just keep thinking what I been telling myself," Longarm went on. "Outlaws're always outlaws, except that the ones hiding behind a badge are worse'n the ones that come right out in the open."

"That's my idea, too," Briggs agreed as they dismounted. He nodded toward the rear of the building. "That's the back door right there. I'll give you time to get in the front, then I'll go in."

"You mean you've still got a key?"

"No. But my boot soles are hard and I'm pretty good at kicking. I'll be inside about two minutes after you are."

"I'll look for you, then. And soon as we're done here we'll hightail over to the land office and see how Julia's coming out."

After the number of visits that she and Clem had made to the land office, Julia's appearance there caused no comment. She nodded and smiled at the two clerks laboring over the cumbersome, fat ledgers that filled the shelf-lined walls of the big outer room, and said to the nearest clerk, "I'd like to take another look at one of the ledgers that my uncle and I have consulted before. The one that has the plats of the Rio Arriba country."

"Of course," the clerk said. "I'll get it for you."

"Don't disturb your work," Julia told him. "I know exactly the one I need to look at and just where it is."

Without waiting for a reply, she moved along the close-spaced rows of shelves filled with oversized ledgers. Though she'd used the land office property registers before, several minutes passed before she found the one that held the detailed maps and descriptions of the land boundaries in the Rio Arriba. Tugging at the massive ledger until she could get both hands on it, Julia carried the big heavy leatherbound book with some difficulty to the small table at the end of the tier of shelves.

Thumbing quickly through the pages she found the one she was seeking. A single glance told her all that she needed to know. The map was not the same as the well-remembered plat she and Clem had consulted several times earlier. It was a larger-scaled version of the map that Carmelita had given her.

Absorbed in the map, Julia had not heard the stealthy approach of Frank Maltby. Her first hint of danger was the sudden pressure of cold steel on the nape of her neck. She recognized Maltby's voice when he whispered in her ear.

"Don't do anything foolish like calling for help, Miss Meadows," he said. "I wouldn't like it if I had to shoot you in here and disturb my clerks, but if you make a disturbance, I'll have no other choice."

"I'm not that stupid," Julia told him. "And I certainly don't intend to give you an excuse for killing me."

"Oh, I don't have any intention of doing that," Maltby assured her. "I wouldn't want to spoil the unpleasant surprise that's waiting for you. Walk ahead of me to my office. There's a gentleman in there who'll be very glad to see you."

With Maltby's pistol pressed into her back and the land agent walking close behind her to hide the gun, Julia walked in front of him to the door of his office. Inside the office, she met the snake-cold stare of Don Esquival

179

Hinojosa. The old man was sitting ramrod stiff in one corner of the room. Maltby poked Julia with the muzzle of his revolver to indicate a chair in the room's opposite corner. She stepped over to it and sat down.

"You have caused me a great deal of inconvenience, Miss Meadows," Don Esquival said. His voice was cold and his black, snakelike eyes glittered malevolently. "And you have caused the loss of some of my most trusted men. I can see only one way for you to repay me for the harm you have done. I will take you with me to my ranch. My men will find ways to amuse themselves with you for a while before you disappear forever."

Longarm halted at the corner of the building that housed the marshal's office and glanced along its side wall. Clem Briggs was standing ready, close to the back door. The two exchanged nods before Longarm stepped around the corner of the building and pushed through the office door.

A single swift sweeping glance told him all that he needed to know. Alberto Espinosa was at the front desk, the desks behind him were occupied by Brady and Chalmers. Both men were occupied with paperwork. Brady was sorting through a stack of warrants, and Chalmers was looking down at a big ledger that he held open in front of him with both hands.

Through the frosted-glass panes of the partition that enclosed Jason Tobin's private cubbyhole, Longarm saw the chief marshal in silhouette leaning forward over his desk, shuffling through a sheaf of papers. Though the three men in the outer office looked up as Longarm entered, none of them spoke.

Without pausing in his leisurely stride Longarm nodded to Espinosa as he passed the young marshal's desk and said under his breath, ''Get ready to dive to the floor. Hell's likely to bust loose in just a minute.''

Ignoring Espinosa's wide-eyed stare of surprise, Longarm stopped in front of Brady's desk, and for the first time could see that the deputy marshal's right arm was in a sling. From the corners of his eyes he saw Chalmers look up from the ledger he was holding in front of him.

Keeping his voice at a conversational level, Longarm said, ''Brady. And you, too, Chalmers. Keep your hands where I can see 'em, because I don't want to have to throw down on you. I'm putting both of you men under arrest.''

Almost before Longarm had finished his announcement, while the two deputies were staring at him with wide-eyed astonishment, a- crash of splintering wood burst form the back of the building and broke the silence. In the few moments that followed the noise the office burst into a spate of activity.

Brady leaped to his feet and began trying clumsily to reach the holstered gun on his right hip with his left hand. Chalmers let the ledger fall to his desk with a thud and dropped his hand to the butt of the holstered revolver at his hip. In his office, Tobin was leaping to his feet.

Longarm did not hesitate. His quick glances had been all that he needed to estimate the odds against him. Swiveling his Colt, he triggered off a shot at Chalmers, whose hand was now on the butt of the revolver on his hip. The heavy .45 slug found its mark. Chalmers's body bucked as it slammed into his chest. For a split second he swayed backward, then his legs gave way and he folded to the floor behind his desk.

Though Longarm heard the two shots that came from Tobin's office in the rear of the room, he ignored them.

Brady had at last managed to draw his pistol. He was raising it for a snapshot when Longarm's second slug smashed into his rib cage and cracked through the bones as though they were cardboard. He reeled as the bullet spun him into a half turn, and though the spasm of his dying reflex closed his finger on the trigger of his weapon, the bullet tore into the top of his desk and raised a small shower of wood slivers.

Longarm turned his eyes toward the frosted glass of Tobin's office just in time to see a shadowy form drop a revolver, sagging as his knees buckled and dropping from sight behind the desk. Longarm strode to the door and threw it open, and through the gunsmoke he could see Clem Briggs lowering his revolver.

Alberto Espinosa's surprised question broke the stillness that followed the fracas. *"Que cosa es?"*

Longarm turned to face the young deputy and said, "I guess the best way to put it is to say them men got their last payoff for selling out." Before Espinosa could reply, he went on, "You take charge here for a little while. Just keep folks from crowding in. Me and Clem's got some business at the land office that's got to be tended to real quick."

Briggs came up to join them as Longarm was speaking. A worried frown crinkled his face and concern was in his voice as he said, "This cleanup job took longer than I thought it would. We didn't get started on it soon enough."

"It ain't more'n a hoot and holler over to the land office," Longarm reminded him. "But you're right, we're a little bit behind time, so let's shake a leg. We'll leave the horses and cut across the square."

"But what am I to do?" Espinosa asked.

"Just stay here and keep everybody but the local law from coming in," Longarm answered. "Me and Clem'll be back soon as we tend to the rest of our business."

As the two men angled across the deserted plaza to the land office, Briggs said, "I sure hope we're not too late. That damned Frank Maltby's as deep into this mess as Tobin was."

Longarm gestured toward the squat adobe building they were approaching and replied, "I don't figure we got too much to worry about, Clem. There ain't been time for anything much to happen to Julia."

"I hope you're right. But he's as deep into this bribing and swindling as Tobin was, and you know what happens to crooks when the law starts closing in on them."

A nod was Longarm's only reply. He'd clamped a cigar between his teeth and was striking a match, and after he'd puffed his stogy into life he said, "I ain't forgetting. But we'll be there in plenty of time."

They reached the land office door, but when they tried to open it found it had been locked. Longarm was beginning to grow alarmed now. He wasted no time. Drawing his Colt, he sent a shot into the lock, shattering it. A kick sent the door swinging open.

Clem Briggs pushed past him to hurry inside. Longarm was a pace behind him as they entered. Over Briggs's shoulder he saw Julia, standing between Maltby and Don Esquival. Don Esquival was raising a silver-plated revolver to Julia's head.

Longarm's Colt seemed to leap into his hand. Before Briggs could free his weapon and while the barrel of Don Esquival's threatening pistol was still well away from its intended target, Longarm sent a bullet whistling into the old hidalgo's chest.

Briggs saw Don Esquival beginning to totter and switched his revolver to cover Frank Maltby. The land agent was bringing up his gun, but Briggs had begun shifting his point of aim just in time to get off the first shot. The hot lead that spurted from his gun's muzzle sped unerringly to its target. Maltby's body jerked as though he'd collided with a speeding locomotive.

While Don Esquival tottered with the impact of Longarm's heavy slug and began to sag downward, his dying reflex cramped his trigger finger tight, but the bullet did no more than tear splinters from the floor.

Maltby was already beginning to fall. The bodies of the pair became partners in death as they'd been in life as they twisted together on the office floor.

"I was afraid you weren't going to get here in time," Julia said. "Don Esquival was in a hurry to get away, and I knew we hadn't even counted on him being here."

"You ain't hurt, are you?" Longarm asked Julia.

"No. But I think I must still be shivering over how close I came to being murdered," she said.

"You'll get over that soon enough," Longarm assured her. "You figure you'll be able to boss them clerks out there for a few minutes?"

"I— I suppose."

"That's what I figured," Longarm said. "You take charge, then. Me and Clem have got to run back to the marshal's office, and he's going to be in charge there like you are here."

"What about you?"

"I'll stay in Santa Fe as long as I can, but if I know Billy Vail, when I send him a wire telling him I closed my case here, he's going to tell me to get on back to Denver. But I don't aim to hurry any more than I have to, because the longer I can push back leaving, the more time you and me will have to spend together.''

Watch for

LONGARM AND THE TEXAS RANGERS

139th novel in the bold LONGARM series
from Jove

Coming in July!